Murder at the Cubbyhole

ALSO BY ALICE ZOGG

Revamp Camp
Final Stop Albuquerque
The Fall of Optimum House
The Lonesome Autocrat
Tracking Backward
Turn the Joker Around
Reaching Checkmate

Murder at the Cubbyhole

Alice Zogg

Aventine Press

This book is a work of fiction.

Published by Aventine Press
55 East Emerson St.
Chula Vista CA, 91911
www.aventinepress.com

ISBN: 1-59330-756-X

Library of Congress Control Number: 2012931894
Library of Congress Cataloging-in-Publication Data
Murder at the Cubbyhole/ Alice Zogg
Printed in the United States of America

In memory of my parents,

Paul and Berta Rutz

CREDITS

A special thank you is due to Hal Sweesy who allowed me a glimpse into the stage world. I so enjoyed your class, Hal! Once again, Gayle Bartos-Pool graciously invited me into her home to give a show-and-tell demonstration of her fabulous handmade Christmas crafts and walked me through the process of creating a 25-inch-tall Santa. Credit for a superb job of editing goes to Valoise Douglas. Her eye for detail is spot on. I could never do without my daughter Franziska, who proofreads my initial manuscript and catches grammatical errors. My gratitude goes to the members of the Los Angeles chapter of Sisters in Crime. I cherish their support and friendship. Last but not least, I applaud my husband, Wilfried, for putting up with my absentmindedness during crucial times in the writing process of this book with the patience of a saint.

CAST OF CHARACTERS

R. A. Huber Private investigator; a lady sleuth par excellence

Peter Huber R. A. Huber's husband; a writer

Antoinette LeJeune (Andi) Huber's assistant; a dynamic young woman

Megan Maguire An actress; had the lead role in the play

Owen Maguire Megan's father; brews beer

Eileen Maguire Megan's mother; grows roses

Amber Pierce Megan's roommate; works at the local gym

Mr. and Mrs. Kingsley Cubbyhole owners; struggling to keep the theater open

Madame Dubois Megan's employer; proprietress of a fashion boutique

Yuri Novokoff Acting instructor; has connections in the theater world

Sal Silverberg Director; his motto is "the show must go on"

Todd Brighton Actor; is full of self-importance

Adriana Rippling	Actress; Megan's understudy
Mercedes Cleveland	Actress; has a true love for acting
Chad Lindhurst	Actor; cast as the character Fortitude in the play
Ralph Weatherford	Theater critic and reviewer; has high standards
Hailey Tuckfield	Megan's longtime best friend; the girl-next-door type
Brent Halifax	An old boyfriend; followed Megan to California
Sergeant John Wolf	Retired Police Officer; asked Huber to investigate the case

Chapter 1

Megan rose to her feet from a kneeling position, lifted her eyes and arms to heaven and proclaimed, "I swear to God and to the world, justice is ultimately served!"

The final curtain of the play *From Sin to Virtue* fell, and tremendous applause thundered through the small playhouse. When it was raised again and the entire cast took a unanimous bow, the enthusiastic audience gave a standing ovation.

A tall and portly man in center-fifth orchestra row scrambled to his feet and cried out, "Amateurs!"

His companion, a small bald man, raising his voice in an effort to be heard over the noise of people clapping, stated, "I liked it."

"A bunch of amateurs," the former insisted, "The characters Vanity and Mother Earth were the only ones worth a damn, until Vanity screwed up her last line!"

"I didn't notice," the bald man murmured as he followed his friend out of the theater.

People shuffled toward the exit of the auditorium as cast members made themselves available in the lobby for a chat with fans.

Minutes later, Megan sat at her dressing table backstage, taking off the heavy stage makeup. She stared at her mirror image, lost in thought. The young woman was well cast as the character Vanity with her hazel eyes, thick dark-brown hair, high cheekbones, 22-inch waist, and a general air of arrogance. *Did I get the point across with my last line? Will anyone even make the connection?*

she wondered. Maybe there's nothing to worry about and I'm just paranoid, she reflected, shrugging off her fear. Then she glanced at the corner table and noticed the pot of exquisite Cattleya orchids with fuchsia and light-pink flowers peeking out of its bright red aluminum foil wrapping. How sweet, a Valentine from a fan, she thought. Searching for a card and finding none, she bent over the orchid pot, reaching deep into its depth.

An ear-piercing explosion shook the dressing room, and her last thought before she left this world was, "They wasted no time!"

Chapter 2

There were four men and two women assembled in their secret meeting place. They had arrived one by one in assigned five-minute intervals, donning their eye masks before they entered, and now sat in their numbered chairs at a long rectangular table, three on each side. Seat number one at the head of the table, reserved for their leader, was empty. The members of the group stayed nameless within that setting and simply referred to themselves as Member One, Two, Three and so forth.

Member Seven asked, "Does anybody know why this special meeting was called?"

No one spoke up.

"Come on, some of you must know! I just flew in this morning. What's up?"

Again, there was no response.

Member Seven was about to press the point further but shut his mouth when the door was pulled open and Member One entered. As he walked to his place at the head of the table with his customary long stride, the rest of the group got to their feet and only sat back down after he did.

There was no question about Member One's mood when he glared at the assembly and said, "I called you here because we have to deal with the stupidity of two of our members." He paused and, staring at Member Five and Six in turn through his eye mask, continued, "I'm referring to the theater episode."

His voice cut like a knife as he went on, "You violated two of our rules. We only acknowledge one another during assignments and in this room. Knowing good and well that contact among our members *outside the job* is forbidden, you did so regardless. On top of that, you broke our non-violence code. You put us all in jeopardy by your pinheaded action."

He turned to Member Five and thundered on, "Did you really think I wouldn't catch on? Let me inform you that all is as plain as day to me! You don't know who I am nor are you familiar with each other's identities, but never forget that I know all about every single one of you down to the last detail."

Member Five said, "We had no choice. She saw - -"

Their leader cut in, "You had tons of better choices than jumping the gun the way you did."

"I tell you, Megan realized that the - -"

"No names, please!"

"Like I said, she got wise to me. I couldn't take the chance of her going to the police; we had to act fast."

Member One exploded, "Without consulting me? How dare you?"

He obviously did not expect an answer and pointing his thin, long finger at Member Six continued, "And *you* couldn't wait to try out your explosives. Both of you are idiots. Sooner or later someone will make the connection. If not the police then somebody else."

Member Six was about to speak up in an attempt at justification, but Member One stretched out his arm in a silencing gesture and stated, "Enough said. Our only option is to lay low for a while. Next month's job is therefore postponed until further notice. Don't forget to leave at your assigned intervals nor remove your masks until after you've exited. Meeting adjourned."

Chapter 3

Six weeks later, R. A. Huber and her husband Peter enjoyed a leisurely evening at their home in Merida, located in the San Fernando Valley at the foot of the Angeles National Forest Mountains. They were sitting at opposite ends of the dining room table, each absorbed with his own project. Peter peered into his laptop screen, doing research for a current manuscript, while his spouse was busy sorting photo prints in chronological order and adding them into an album. After over four decades of marriage, the couple felt comfortable spending long periods of time in close proximity without uttering a single word.

Regula suddenly broke the silence and said, "Guess who took me to lunch today?"

Peter looked up, slightly disoriented, "Hmm?"

"Remember Sergeant Wolf?"

"Of the South Pasadena Police Department?"

"Yes, him. He called me out of the blue and we met for lunch."

"How is he these days?"

"Getting older like the rest of us. He still looks impressive, though."

"So why did he want to see you?"

"He had a favor to ask."

Peter chuckled, making his graying mustache wriggle, and said, "That's a switch; you're usually the one to ask favors of the police."

"Sergeant Wolf is retired now. He wants me to investigate a murder case."

"You're kidding!"

"Nope. Want to hear about it?"

"Sure," he replied, "I'm at a dead-end in my research, so shoot." He shut down his computer, leaned back, folded his hands behind his white head of hair, and was ready to listen.

His wife said, "Remember the news around Valentine's Day about an explosion at the Cubbyhole Theater, killing a young actress?"

"Yes, I sure do."

"Her name was Megan Maguire and she is a distant relative of the Sergeant. The police are investigating but so far have not made much progress, and Megan's parents begged Sergeant Wolf to look into it. He doesn't feel right about meddling since he's no longer on the force and suggested that they hire me. The way he put it, 'This case is right up your alley, Mrs. Huber.'"

"Well Regula, what case isn't?" Peter teased.

His spouse ignored the remark and related all she had learned during her luncheon that day. Sergeant Wolf still had connections and was able to give her plenty of information.

"Evidently, the explosion had been caused by a device hidden inside a potted orchid arrangement that was delivered to the actress's backstage dressing room. The entire room and part of the adjacent hallway was destroyed, and there was hardly anything left of the flower pot for analysis. Since the bomb, or whatever explosive device was used, self-destructed, there was no evidence of how exactly it had been activated. The assumption is that there was either a timer attached or most likely the device was set in motion by a cell phone.

"Consequently, the young lady perished. At least the Sergeant was positive that her end came swiftly. Megan was 22 years old, a college dropout, born and raised in

Portland, Oregon of Irish immigrant parents. She moved to Southern California in search of an acting career. She shared an apartment with another young woman in Pasadena and supported herself as a salesclerk at an upscale fashion boutique. The young woman took acting lessons and joined an amateur theater group where she landed the lead role in *From Sin to Virtue*."

Peter said, "The play sounds familiar, but I can't place it."

"We saw it a long time ago on Broadway during a visit to New York. It centers on the seven capital vices and virtues."

"Oh, I remember now; it was an excellent show."

She explained that Mr. Wolf had given her the names of all the people the police interviewed. The list was long, starting with Megan's parents, several theater group members, the acting school instructor, the proprietress of *Le Monde Fashion* where she worked, her roommate, and an old discarded boyfriend who had followed her to the Southland.

Coming to the end of her narrative she said, "That's it in a nutshell."

"You've got your work cut out for you; if you're taking the case, that is," Peter remarked.

"You bet I'm taking it. Sergeant Wolf helped me out a lot in the past. The Worthington file comes to mind and another at North Shore Lake Tahoe where my investigation took us all over Central Mexico."

"As I recall, we had a great time on that trip!"

"Don't get me off the subject, Peter. Like I said, Wolf held my hand more than once, the least I can do now is try giving his relatives some closure." She added, "Besides, getting a taste of the acting world might be interesting."

"Is it a pro bono job?"

"I offered, but Megan's folks, the Maguires, insisted on paying for my services."

Peter raised an eyebrow and said, "You already talked to the victim's parents?"

"When I got back to my office after lunch, Sergeant Wolf put through a three-way call to me and the Maguires in Portland."

"Are you going to let Andi help you with the investigation?"

"Probably, unless she's too busy studying for her semester finals."

Regula had kept up her photo project while talking, and now she closed the album with a bang and said, "Done!"

Chapter 4

Antoinette LeJeune, known to her friends as Andi, was riding her Harley-Davidson from Santa Monica to R. A. Huber's office in Pasadena. At three in the afternoon, traffic was already advancing toward a peak on this Friday at the end of March. Thankfully, as a motorcyclist, she could use the diamond lane. Plus, she had perfect weather for riding, with not a cloud in the sky and temperatures in the upper seventies. Andi would not have traded her Harley for any luxury car. No way!

After making the transition from the 405 North Freeway to the 118 East, traffic eased a tad and Andi let her mind roam. She thought of the different places she had called home in the last three and a half years. At eighteen, following the passing of her Daddy, she had ridden to California on his Harley. The bike was not her only inheritance. Daddy also left her three pieces: a hunting rifle which she sold to a pawn shop before hitting the road, a Derringer and a Stinger pen pistol, both still in her possession. Besides his individual savings, Daddy had set up a college fund for her, and the sale of his bar and property in New Orleans had brought her additional cash, which kept her above water so far.

In the first few months as a newcomer, she had stayed with her kinfolk, Auntie Sue and Uncle Earl, in Pasadena. Then she had briefly lived in a one-bedroom apartment in Century City, proudly calling it the very first place of her own. She smiled to herself as she thought back to her dog-walking days. Andi would never forget the day Mrs. Huber called her with a job offer as assistant sleuth, taking her up on a plea she had made on impulse several months before. She had been thrilled at the chance to prove herself as an undercover detective and rode up to the Big Bear area where she took residency at Optimum House.

After that initial job, she was a steady helper to her detective boss. In order to be closer to Pasadena City College and also R. A. Huber's office, she soon moved back in with her kinfolk. Last fall, when she transferred to UCLA, she had accepted Mr. and Mrs. Huber's offer of the guestroom at their house in Merida, and although her short stay with them had been fun, the commute to UCLA proved too much. So now she was back in West L.A., sharing an apartment with two other students. For a girl who lived with her Daddy in the same house in New Orleans from the day she was born and lost her momma until reaching the age of eighteen, she surely had gotten around lately!

Andi was riding along the 210 Freeway now and would shortly arrive at her destination. Busy with her studies, she had not seen her boss in over a month and was full of enthusiasm about getting briefed on Mrs. Huber's new case. Until that very moment, she had not realized how much she missed her fearless, intelligent, athletic yet elegant employer with the salt-and-pepper hair and Swiss accent. They teased one another about their "non-existing" accents, neither admitting to having one. In the three years of working for Mrs. Huber, she had not only come to respect and admire her employer, but had grown fond of her.

As she approached the two-story office building in Pasadena and rode into the parking lot, Andi wondered what kind of new mystery her boss had for them to solve.

Chapter 5

R. A. Huber glanced up from her notes when Andi blew into her office like a whirlwind. The young woman crossed the room with a few long steps, placed her helmet at the opposite side of the desk from where Huber's Staunton Rosewood chessboard was set up with the chessmen, and plopped into the client chair. Although Andi had intellectually grown in the last three years, she was hardly changed physically. Long-legged at 5'9" and weighing about 120 pounds, her wavy auburn hair cascaded down her shoulders in the same unruly way, and she still looked at the world with mischievous green eyes. As was typical for her, she was clad in jeans, a black leather jacket, and cowboy boots.

Andi said, "How you doin', Mrs. Huber? I'm tickled pink about your lettin' me help solve another case!"

"Studying seems to agree with you; you look great!"

"Thank you, ma' am!"

Getting down to business Huber said, "Let me clue you in," and told all she knew about the Megan Maguire killing, occasionally consulting her notes in order to go into more detail.

Andi listened carefully, and when her boss's briefing came to a halt, asked, "So Megan's folks are no longer here?"

"That's right. They drove down to see their daughter perform, making a vacation trip out of the occasion. After the tragedy, they stayed in Southern California another ten days and then went home to Portland, taking their only child's ashes along with them."

Andi tried not to dwell on that sad picture and said, "I reckon the police checked where the orchid came from."

"They certainly did, but it got them nowhere. The delivery person used a bogus florist name claiming he was from - -" she consulted her paperwork, "- - Champion Arrangements, dropping off flowers for Megan. It turns out that Champion Arrangements does not exist. The authorities investigated florists throughout Pasadena and beyond, but their inquiries dead-ended. Countless purchases of orchids were made all over Southern California on that Valentine's Day weekend, so they could have been bought anywhere, and not just at a flower shop. Orchids are also available at supermarkets and places like Trader Joe's around holidays, especially Valentine's Day. For all we know, the villain could have grown them in his own backyard. And needless to say, the orchid deliverer was not identified."

Huber absentmindedly lifted a white rook from its position on the chessboard, and twirling it around in her fingers, said, "According to the information given to Sergeant Wolf, the Cubbyhole was full to capacity the night of that performance; it was the play's premiere. If the device was activated by a cell phone in the audience, conducting the investigation from that angle would be a waste of time."

"I've lost you, boss."

"The task to check out each and every person who sat in that theater would be impossible."

"Gotcha!"

"And even if it was set off by a timer, there was nothing left of it to analyze."

Andi said, "So are the police clueless as to suspects?"

"I wouldn't say that. Their investigation is still on-going, but according to the Maguires, the police have not come up with any serious suspects yet."

"It *was* murder, right?"

"Placing a bomb in the Cubbyhole would definitely suggest homicidal intent. The explosion was most likely meant to kill Megan and no one else, but it's too early to jump to that conclusion."

"I hear ya."

Huber shoved a piece of paper across the desk, saying, "Here are the individuals the police have questioned. We'll soon begin our own interviewing."

Andi looked at the long list of names and addresses and asked, "Which ones are mine to tackle?"

"When are your semester finals over?"

"Not until next Wednesday, but I can - -"

"No, you can't, Andi! Your education is top priority. I will conduct the investigation alone for the first few days. Then, by the end of next week, I'll assign people for you to interview."

Andi knew better than to argue the point.

Chapter 6

At eleven o'clock on Saturday morning, R. A. Huber stood on the sidewalk and looked up at the building with large lettering across its façade: Pine Forest Apartments. Shaking her head, she paused before ascending the exterior stairs to apartment number 9C on the second floor. There were neither pines nor forests anywhere near the apartment complex, located a short distance away from Pasadena City College.

Loud music was sounding from apartment 9C and she had to ring the doorbell twice before being heard. When the door finally flew open, Huber was looking at a slightly out of breath young woman with sharp features and hair pulled back into a pony tail. She was barefoot, wearing an athletic bra and exercise shorts, barely covering her buttocks.

"Amber Pierce? I'm R. A. Huber."

"Oh, is it eleven already?" Amber asked, her breathing returning to normal. "Come on in."

She pushed the "off" button on the CD remote, pointed to the only available chair in the room, and said, "Have a seat. I was choreographing a new aerobic dance routine." She cleared away one corner of the sofa piled with laundry, and flopped herself down.

Huber asked, "You work at a local gym, correct?"

"That's right. It's just around the corner. I teach aerobic fitness classes and am also a personal trainer."

"I can see that you're a good role model for your clientele; you look perfectly fit!"

"Thank you!"

"Now let's get to the reason I came to see you."

Amber said, "Like I mentioned on the phone and already told the police weeks ago, I didn't know Megan well. We were just roomies."

"That is actually a plus."

"What?"

"Not having been close, perhaps you can give me a more objective account of the kind of young woman she was."

"I guess so. And since you're asking, let me tell you, she wasn't the easiest person to live with. Stuck-up is what I'd have called her. You couldn't keep a real conversation going as she walked around the place forever practicing her lines. Every morning she hogged the bathroom, getting herself all dolled up before going to work. Worst of all, she was a neat freak. If I left anything sitting around without putting it away in what she considered 'its proper place', she tossed it in the trash."

Huber glanced around the messy room and remarked, "I take it that your present roommate is not plagued by neatness."

Amber stated, "I haven't found a replacement yet." And she could not hide the resentment in her voice when she added, "Megan left me stranded and I have to come up with the rent money all by myself."

"Did she have many friends?"

"Not real friends; she mostly hung around her theater group crowd. She did call and text an old girlfriend in Portland a lot, though."

"Any boyfriends?"

"When she first moved in, a guy hung around, but she wasn't interested."

"Do you know his name?"

"I can't remember."

"Anyone else?"

"She had lots of admirers and dated some of them. Megan was good looking, I grant her that."

"But no one serious?"

"Not that I'd noticed."

"How long have you known Megan?"

"Two years."

"So the two of you found this apartment to share?"

"Oh please! I've been renting here for four years and had other roommates before her. I just put an ad in the local paper, you know, 'Room for rent.'"

Huber said, "Now tell me what you know about what happened on the evening of the premiere at the Cubbyhole Theater."

"I have nothing to tell. The explosion was as much of a shock to me as to everyone else."

"Were you there?"

"Sure. Megan talked of nothing else for days, so I felt pressured to see the play."

"Did you enjoy it?"

"What a morbid thing for you to ask!" she answered, clearly offended.

"I meant before the explosion."

"Oh! Yes, I did like the stage performance of *From Sin to Virtue*. I'll admit Megan was really good as Vanity."

"Was her behavior different that day or the days before the opening of the play?"

"She was excited and a bit nervous, but otherwise her usual arrogant self."

"Do you think she was frightened of anyone?"

"No, and if she was, she wouldn't tell me. As you figured, we weren't that close."

"Did you hear the explosion?"

"It was hardly a thing you could've avoided hearing and feeling the vibrations from."

"Where exactly were you when the blast hit?"

"I was just coming back from the ladies room and we were on our way out of the theater when we heard the explosion. We hit the floor, covering our heads with both arms, thinking it was either an earthquake or a holdup."

"Who is 'we'?"

"Me and my boyfriend. I'm sure he doesn't want to get involved, so I'd rather not give you his name."

"Did Megan have any enemies?"

Amber thought about it for a moment before she answered, "I imagine that she was a pain in the neck to many people, but I can't see that anybody hated her enough to want to murder her."

"Do you have a theory as to the incident at the Cubbyhole?"

"Maybe the bomb was meant to kill someone else and was placed in the wrong spot. The target might have been somewhere else backstage or even sitting among the spectators."

"That's an idea. I'll keep it in mind."

R. A. Huber got up to leave and said, "Thank you for your time. And good luck with finding a new roommate."

Before she was halfway down the stairs, she could hear the music blaring out of Amber's apartment again.

Chapter 7

On her way out of the Pine Forest Apartments, Huber walked by the tenant's laundromat, located in a separate small structure. The door to it stood open and she heard the noise of washers and dryers in use. On a whim, she stuck her head in. There were three people in the place, tending to their laundry.

She asked, "By chance, did any of you know your neighbor Megan Maguire in apartment 9C?"

Two people shook their heads and squeezed by her with their baskets full of clothing.

Huber was about to retreat too, when the third person, a young man, looked up from folding his towels and said, "Would that be the fitness nut who blasts her audio and jumps around, making the building shake?"

"You've got the correct apartment, but I meant her roommate."

"Oh, you mean the beauty. But she - -" he caught himself and continued " - - no longer lives there."

His slight hesitation was not lost on Huber and she prompted, "So you do know what happened to her."

The young man eyed her with caution and said, "Are you a relative of hers?"

"You don't have to worry about my feelings in the matter; I'm a private investigator, looking into Megan's case."

He scrutinized her from head to toe, then looked all around them and said, "Where's the hidden camera?"

She reached into her purse and handed him one of her business cards.

He glanced at it and blurted, "R. A. Huber, Private Investigator. Damn right; you *are* a private eye! I thought it was a joke."

"Now that we've got that straight, what do you know about Megan Maguire?"

"Not much. Just that she was killed."

"Who told you?"

"I learned about it indirectly."

He didn't elaborate and seemed to concentrate on folding his laundry.

Huber took a step toward him, crossed her arms and waited.

"Okay, I'll tell you," he finally said, "I wasn't really eavesdropping; just came to drop off my rent check at the superintendent's office, when I realized that he was talking to the cops."

"So what did you accidentally overhear?"

"That the woman in 9C was killed at the Cubbyhole Theater. I heard about the explosion on the news, but had no idea the person who died was actually my neighbor."

"How well did you know Megan?"

"I didn't know her at all."

"May I ask how long you've lived here?"

"Close to a year."

Huber casually walked over to the small window, and, looking out asked, "Which is your building?"

"I live in building C."

"That's right; you mentioned that the building shakes when the young lady practices her aerobic routines. So your place is on the ground floor?"

"No, on the second, apartment 10C."

In a swift motion Huber turned away from the window and wagging her finger at him said, "Apartment 10C is next door to where Megan lived. Don't tell me you've never met her over the span of a year!"

His face turned red as he protested, "Naturally I saw her coming and going, but we didn't socialize. When I first moved in, both women came to my door together and introduced themselves as Amber and Megan, but I could never remember which was which."

"When was the last time you saw Megan, to put it in your words, coming and going?"

He thought about it for a second and then said, "It was the Friday right before Valentine's Day."

"And that day sticks in your mind?"

"Not really. It wasn't until later when hearing the cop say she was killed on Saturday that I realized I'd seen her the night before."

"Did you talk to her?"

"Yeah, it was weird. Even though we didn't really know each other, she usually smiled and commented about the weather or something when we crossed paths."

"And on that evening she was different?"

"Exactly. Like I said, it was strange. We were both coming home around eleven at night and she was standing in front of her door, fiddling for keys in her purse. I said, 'Good night, sleep tight,' as I passed by her on the way to my place next door. I obviously had startled her; she seemed scared out of her mind and almost fainted. The building is well lit at night and when recognizing me, she seemed to pull herself together. I asked whether she was okay and she assured me that all was fine."

"Granted, you frightened her, but I see nothing strange in that."

"I'm getting to it. After she found her keys, and just before she opened the door and went inside, she did something like this - -" he first touched his forehead with his right hand, then the middle of his chest, then left and right.

"She crossed herself?"

He nodded. "She did it slowly and deliberately. It was dramatic."

Chapter 8

On Monday morning, R. A. Huber had an appointment to meet with Mr. and Mrs. Kingsley, the owners of the Cubbyhole Theater, at their playhouse. It was located down a side alley off the main drag in Old Town Pasadena. She was a few minutes early and found the place locked. From the outside, the small theater could have been mistaken for an office building were it not for the wide front portal. Photos with scenes from the current play were exhibited in glass cases on either side of the entrance. Huber was studying a picture of a young woman in the role of Vanity when the couple walked up to her. They were both well into their seventies. Huber had the distinct feeling that the pair had been arguing moments before but were trying to hide this from her.

After introductions were made, she pointed to the photo and asked, "Was this Megan Maguire?"

Mrs. Kingsley replied, "Oh no, it's the actress who replaced her. Considering what happened, I think it would be in poor taste to show a picture of the first Vanity."

Mr. Kingsley unlocked the entry and then pulled the heavy doors open. As Huber followed them past the ticketing counter into the lobby, he said, "Have you been to our theater before?"

"I sure have on several occasions," Huber replied with an appreciative smile. "I enjoyed the small scale setting as it gave me an intimate rapport with the performers. You have a real treasure here."

Flattered, he beamed at her. Then he said, "There's an office to the left where we can talk," and led the way past the coat check and restrooms.

To call the tiny workstation an office was a generous statement. Mr. Kingsley motioned Huber into the only comfortable chair behind the modest desk and opened up two folding chairs for him and his wife he found leaning against the wall. The only other furniture was an old-fashioned wooden file cabinet. The small space had no window, just three walls and an open arched entryway. There was no computer, printer, or fax machine in the room.

He said, "You're not claustrophobic, are you?"

"Don't worry, I'm not," Huber replied. "First off, let me thank you both for granting me this interview. Since you were questioned by the police a while back, some of the material we'll go over might be repetitive."

Mr. Kingsley said, "We're glad to help and the faster the culprit is caught, the better."

"Do you folks run the theater yourselves?"

"We used to when we were younger, but decided to hire a manager some years back." And with a meaningful side glance toward his wife he remarked, "As we're learning now, it is not always a good idea to delegate one's responsibilities." Returning his attention back to Huber he continued, "This is his office."

"Would he know about deliveries made to the backstage area?"

"You mean props and such?"

"No, I was thinking of things sent to actors; like the orchids delivered to Megan Maguire, for instance."

"Oh, I see, how stupid of me! Our manager takes care of the business aspect of the theater, but the director might know which of the stagehands accepted the flowers."

"Would that be Sal Silverberg?"

"Correct."

Mrs. Kingsley chimed in, "He is a tremendous asset to the cast. We are so lucky to have him."

Huber said, "I have Mr. Silverberg on my list of people to see." Then she asked, "I take it you've owned the theater for a long time?"

"35 years, and we're quite nostalgic about it," said Mrs. Kingsley.

Her spouse nodded and said, "The Cubbyhole was already old when we bought it and in dire need of repairs. When it was put on the market we feared that if sold to the wrong people, the memorable playhouse would be torn down. We couldn't let that happen and put in a generous bid."

Huber remarked, "You were lucky to be able to do that."

"You've got that right. Just around the time the theater was for sale, we'd inherited a substantial sum and planned to invest it in real estate. We were, and still are, performing arts enthusiasts and eagerly grabbed the opportunity to keep this place alive. There was even money left for repairs and remodeling."

The sadness in Mrs. Kingsley's voice was undeniable as she said, "Those were the good old days. In the current economy it is a daily struggle to keep our doors open."

"Now, don't whine, dear," her husband put in. "*From Sin to Virtue* is a success. We are nearly sold out at every performance."

"You keep the play going despite what happened to Megan?"

He replied, "We initially thought to close down the Cubbyhole for a while, but the director insisted that the show must go on and has replaced her with the understudy." And with a bit of embarrassment he added, "The news of what happened backstage on the night of the debut performance seems to have put our little theater into the limelight. As I mentioned, we've had a full house ever since."

His wife commented, "There is no harm in seizing a good business opportunity, now is there?"

Mr. Kingsley gave her an irritated look and she quickly added, "After the explosion we hired extra security personnel, though."

"Are there other performances at the Cubbyhole besides *From Sin to Virtue?*"

"Oh yes," she said. "Something's going on almost every night; we have to be flexible, or else couldn't survive." She turned to her husband and asked, "Do you know this week's schedule?"

"Let me think - - Mondays are usually dark. I believe tomorrow is improv night; Wednesdays are play rehearsals; on Thursday we'll have a magic show; and if I'm not mistaken, there is a chamber music concert on Friday. And of course, the play is Saturday and Sunday nights."

"How well did you know Megan?"

They glanced at one another sideways and replied in unison, "We didn't know her."

Huber stared at them.

Mrs. Kingsley explained, "We saw her on stage at the dress rehearsal and also on opening night, but we'd never talked to her."

"I see. Was she a good actress?"

"Indeed she was and played an impressionable Vanity."

"Did Megan have a dressing room all to herself, or did she share it with others?"

"She used the small dressing room which accommodates only one person."

"How bad was the damage to it?"

Her husband took over and stated, "It was completely destroyed and so was part of the hallway. We had to get estimates and last Friday finally obtained the okay from the insurance company to go ahead with the reconstruction. Work on it will start next week."

"So the crime scene is still untouched?"

"It's boarded up." He got to his feet and beckoned, "Come, I'll show you."

Mrs. Kingsley said, "You two go ahead; looking at the destruction gives me the willies."

Mr. Kingsley turned the auditorium lights on and then led her down the right-hand side aisle. As they passed by rows of seats covered in red velvet fabric, Huber got a glimpse of the heavy brocade curtain drawn across the proscenium style stage, before they mounted the few steps leading backstage.

Mr. Kingsley suddenly became a tour guide and said, "We are now passing through the green room, a lounge where performers wait when they are not needed onstage. On the opposite side is the dimmer room housing the dimmer racks which provide power to the lighting rig in the theater."

Stepping a few yards down the hallway he continued, "To your right is a storage room, and next to it the male dressing room with adjoining restroom. On the left we have the female dressing room and corresponding restroom. The door adjacent to it leads to the back entrance."

Then they walked a few more paces down the corridor and without warning came upon an area barricaded off by plywood panels, and beyond, nothing but a big gaping hole.

He said, "As you can see, there's nothing left of the room and this part of the hallway."

Huber peered into the abyss for a long moment, and then said, "Why was there an additional dressing room needed in such a small theater?"

"How perceptive of you! Originally, the room used to be another storage room to hold costumes, wigs and props. A few years back, we had a famous star among the cast - - I won't mention her name - - with a big ego, demanding to have her own private dressing room. As a courtesy to her, we converted the little storage place into a dressing room and then kept it that way. The lead ladies have had their private place backstage ever since."

They turned away from the gloomy site and retraced their steps. As they passed the back entrance, Huber asked, "So the orchid plant was delivered through this door and brought to where there's nothing but a ruin now?"

"I would guess so."

There was no point in lingering backstage any longer. They returned to the auditorium, walked through it, and headed back to the small office where Mrs. Kingsley still sat on the same folding chair. She seemed a bit muddled, and Huber suspected that the lady might have dozed off and was now trying hard to focus.

"I have just one more question. Do either of you have a theory as to why the young woman was killed?"

Mr. Kingsley shook his head and replied, "I can't imagine why anyone would do such an atrocious deed."

His wife said, "The modern world is full of violence and criminals; no place is safe anymore."

"Evil has always existed in our world, and always will," Huber stated.

Chapter 9

On that same afternoon, R. A. Huber was scheduled to see Madame Dubois, owner of *Le Monde Fashion*. The upscale boutique was located in South Pasadena on a cul-de-sac. The establishments on that particular street were comparable to those of Rodeo Drive, serving a wealthy clientele. The lady detective had on occasion done a bit of window shopping in the area, but never ventured into any of the places. *Le Monde Fashion* was well-known for its clever window displays. Huber remembered having strolled along the district one day in December and being captivated by the ingenious holiday window exhibit. In the foreground, there stood one single mannequin dressed in a red floor-length cape, and an enormous star loomed over the entire background space. The star sparkled with such brilliance that it attracted people's attention clear across the street.

She now admired another fascinating window scene. A cardboard dummy dressed in a police officer's uniform had a whistle squeezed between his lips, and with an outstretched arm held off traffic to let three mannequins parade by. Each was decked out in a different color outfit, with matching hat, purse, sunglasses and coordinated jewelry.

As soon as Huber stepped inside the shop, a tall, stunning young woman walked up to her and announced, "Welcome to *Le Monde Fashion*," and with a trained eye took in the potential customer's appearance. Huber, although dressed in her usual chic mode, was out of her league in this establishment.

The young woman said, "May I help you?"

"I have an appointment to see Madame Dubois. My name is R. A. Huber."

"Oh sure, Ms. Huber, I'll tell her you're here," and she vanished.

Left alone, Huber looked around. The place was not busy. She spotted a lone customer at the opposite end of the store browsing through suits with the help of another salesclerk, equally attractive as the young woman who had welcomed her. Huber scrutinized a few items hanging from a clothes rack near her, noting that the stylish garments were of superior quality, and she was not surprised to find no price tags attached.

Her escort suddenly stood next to her again and said, "This way, please," and she followed her out the store to the back corridor. They passed several doors and at the end of the hallway came to a halt in front of an area similar to a small hotel lobby. The young woman asked her to have a seat and then left.

Huber barely had time to select one of the upholstered chairs and glance around the place when she heard a door being shut and then fast approaching footsteps. A second later, a forty-year-old petite brunette entered the area with a brisk gait. She was clad in black leggings and a loose black-and-grey tunic and wore dark flats resembling ballet slippers. Her hair was pulled into a ponytail, and she wore no jewelry or any kind of makeup. In short, the woman looked more like an artist than the proprietress of an upscale fashion boutique.

Huber stood up, and at 5'6" towered over the other woman by several inches.

"Voilà Madame Huber," she said, in an unmistakable French accent.

The lady detective said, *"Bon après-midi Madame Dubois. Merci de prendre le temps de me reçevoir."*

"Pas de problème. Vous êtes canadienne-française?"

"Non, je suis de la Suisse."

As they both sat down, the conversation reverted to English and Madame Dubois said, "Excuse my getup; I'm in the middle of creating my next window display."

Astonished, Huber asked, "You're doing the window dressing yourself?"

"I enjoy it. Besides, I wouldn't trust anyone else with the job."

"You are extremely talented."

Then she got to the point and said, "As I mentioned on the phone, Megan Maguire's parents hired me to investigate her homicide. Losing a child is hard enough, but adding the cruel act of murder is unbearable. I can't imagine how I'd cope if it was one of my kids."

"I'm not a mother, but feel for Megan's family."

"How long did Megan work for you?"

"About two years."

"What are the requirements for hiring sales personnel for your establishment?"

"You mean education-wise?"

"No, I meant what are you looking for in an employee?"

Madame Dubois's mannerism became extremely French when she answered, "My collections are not for the masses. I am fortunate to count on a small elite clientele. Each season, my customers tend to buy their entire wardrobe at *Le Monde Fashion*. We provide private modeling for them, if desired. To answer your question, my salesgirls need to have a sense of fashion, be discreet, friendly, honest, and able to take care of the shop while I'm busy elsewhere. It is also important that they look presentable and preferably be tall, so I can use them as models."

"What do you mean by 'discreet'?"

"My customers are like loyal old friends, and many of them are famous. What they tell us goes no farther than these walls."

"I see." And with a sweeping gesture encircling their surroundings she asked, "And this is the area where the modeling takes place?"

"*Certainement.*"

"Was Megan a competent employee?"

"Yes, she did a good job and was reliable. She had great looks and carried herself well. Many of my regular customers asked for her in particular when they wanted outfits modeled."

"Did she act differently or seem afraid in the days before her tragic death?"

"I did not notice anything like that."

"Was she friends with the other sales staff?"

"I only had one other sales clerk besides Megan. Angie, the young woman who showed you in just now, is new. And, no, Megan kept to herself."

"Am I correct in presuming that you've lived in the States for many years?"

"Twenty-two, to be exact."

"Is your husband also French?"

"My Robert was a born American."

"Was?"

"I became a bride at 20 and a widow at 21."

"So sorry to hear that."

Madame Dubois brushed it off with the flip of her hand. "It was long ago. Robert served in the first Gulf War in Operation Desert Storm. Even though there were a relatively small amount of American casualties, Robert was one of the unlucky few killed by enemy fire."

"The reason I assumed that your spouse was French is because of your name."

"Oh, I went back to my maiden name when starting *Le Monde Fashion*. Robert's name was Nelson."

"Dubois certainly has a more authentic ring."

They sat in silence for a moment while Huber reflected on what to ask the lady next. She finally said, "How did you find out about what happened to Megan?"

"Pardon?"

"Did you read it in the paper or did you first learn the news from the police?"

"I knew right away."

"You mean you were there at the Cubbyhole Theater to watch Megan perform?"

"Not just her. My boyfriend is also one of the actors in the play."

Huber raised her eyebrows and said, "Oh, who is that?"

Madame Dubois said, "Chad Lindhurst. He is the character Fortitude in the play."

Then she continued, "When I heard the explosion coming from backstage, I was paralyzed for a moment. As soon as I could move again, I ran there in panic, thinking that my boyfriend might be hurt. There was chaos all around, but I finally spotted Chad and he told me that Megan's dressing room was completely blown to pieces with her in it."

"So by coincidence one of your salesclerks and your boyfriend acted on the same stage?"

"It was no coincidence. Chad has belonged to an amateur theater group for years. One day Megan told me that she was taking acting lessons and would like to get experience on stage, so I had Chad put a good word in for her with the director of *From Sin to Virtue*. She auditioned and got the lead part."

"Do you have any idea who could have wanted to harm Megan?"

"No, I can't imagine. Some of the other performers could have been jealous, but surely not to the point of wanting to kill her. She was a bit self-important which was only natural considering her looks and talent."

"She *was* talented then?"

"Chad thought so, and I did too."

Huber could think of nothing else to ask and let the woman resume her window dressing.

Chapter 10

Peter swallowed the last bite of salmon and said, "You're an excellent cook when you put your mind to it!"

"Meaning my mind is mostly elsewhere?" his spouse replied with a smirk.

Minutes later they lingered over coffee and she said, "I called Andi to keep her posted on the interviews I've held so far. Her last final is Wednesday morning and then she's free to help me with the investigation."

Peter asked, "So how's it going?"

"I've got some interesting information from the people I've seen, but it's way too early to form an opinion."

"Tell me about the folks you've talked to."

So she did just that, starting with Amber Pierce and ending with Madame Dubois.

Peter paid keen attention and when she came to a halt in her narrative, he asked, "What is Amber like?"

"If you mean to look at, she has a horse face with a lean body."

"A horse face?"

"Sure, there are two basic types of human faces; baby faces and horse faces."

"I learn something new every day! But what I really wanted to know is what kind of a young woman did she strike you as?"

"I got the impression that Amber was not sensitive, but honest. For example, she had no problem telling me of her gripes with Megan. In fact, she was vexed that her roommate had the nerve to die, leaving her with the entire rent check due."

Peter said, "She seems emotionless."

"Or extremely clever."

He gave her a puzzled look but then caught on. "Oh, I see. She might have been using reverse psychology on you." Then he asked, "What did you think of the Kingsleys?"

"On the surface the old couple was rather sweet. I believe they purchased the Cubbyhole for the love of the performing arts. They're struggling to keep the place running, though."

"I thought you said that the play is doing well."

"*From Sin to Virtue* seems to be a success, but how long can that last?"

"You're right, that won't help them in the long run. What did you mean by 'On the surface the couple was sweet'? Are you suggesting that they're a fake?"

"Not really, they just acted a bit strange, but it was probably all in my imagination. For all I know they could have had a fight just before meeting with me and tried to hide their emotions."

Then he remarked, "The owner of *Le Monde Fashion* sounds interesting. What's her name again?"

"Madame Dubois."

"Does she want people to believe her fashions come straight from Paris when in fact they're made in China?"

"I had a close look at a few of her garments, and I'd say made in Italy would be a better guess."

"So she's on the level?"

"I made sure that she's not an imposter."

"How so?"

"Let's just say that her French is better than mine."

Regula got up and, clearing the coffee cups away, said, "What did you think of the bit of news I picked up from Amber's neighbor in the laundry room?"

"You mean about Megan making the sign of the cross?"
"That's right."

"In my opinion that's only natural. The young woman was Irish, so it makes sense that she crossed herself and thanked God when she realized that she was safe after being frightened to death."

"Correct, but you're missing the point. Like you say, she was *frightened to death*. So far, every person I've interviewed told me that Megan did not act differently and was not worried or afraid, but what that young man saw her do is proof to me that she had reason to be scared."

Chapter 11

At that exact time, 20 miles east of the Huber residence, two employees were setting up a conference room at a Pasadena hotel. They arranged seven chairs around the rectangular table and then tagged each with its corresponding number, starting at the head with number one. Every first Monday evening of each month, hotel personnel went through the same routine of getting the place ready.

While placing two pitchers filled with ice water and seven glasses on the table, one of them said, "Hey Carlos, do you know what kind of weirdoes hold these meetings?"

"What makes you think they're weirdoes?" his co-worker replied. "I've never met any of them. You know the rule; after setting up, we get lost."

"Don't you think by now they'd find their chair without a number on it?"

"Maybe they're not the same people every month. How should I know?"

"Who are they anyhow?"

"My guess is they belong to some kind of religious organization or maybe even a cult. Or they could be members of a secret society club. It's none of our business."

"Let's play a trick on them and switch the numbers around!"

"We'd better not if we want to keep our jobs." Then he looked at his watch and said, "Let's get out of here; they'll start showing up at any moment."

Two hours later, the meeting was coming to an end and Member One said, "So we're clear on every detail. I'll be there to make decisions should we have to improvise on the spur of the moment." He tucked his notes into his briefcase and said, "Meeting over. Make sure all of you check for the green light before getting to the site."

Members Two through Seven filed out of the conference room at the prescribed intervals to avoid contact with one another on the outside. In the end, Member One was left alone to linger in his chair.

He removed his eye mask and reflected on how it all started. Initially, it had been nothing but a vague idea in his head and then it became a challenge to prove that he could mastermind and organize the stunts. He had carefully selected his members and then planned the very first job, almost as a hobby. Soon it became an addiction and they were striking out once a month. It had been going on well over a year now and so far they were getting away with it. He attributed their success to the fact that all members had responsible day jobs and none had a criminal record. When adding Member Six to the team, he'd had reservations. Granted, Member Six's expertise benefited the group, but he should never have allowed that particular member to join since the person was introduced by Member Five. The reason his operation worked so well was because the members had no connection to one another in their everyday lives.

Early on, one of the members had proposed leaving a toy monkey figure hanging by its tail at each scene. Personally, he thought the gesture was childish, but most of the others had applauded the idea and suggested making it their signature. It was such a minor detail that he gave in and let them have their monkeys.

Admittedly, even divided by seven, the payoff from the jobs was worthwhile, but the main attraction for him - - and he was pretty sure also for the rest of his crew - - was the thrill and danger they could expect anew at every site.

Nothing compared to the adrenaline rush and frisson at the crucial moments of each heist. A quick smile came over his face as he thought of his wife. She had been asking a lot of questions lately and seemed more and more intrigued by his unexplained absences on many nights and his absent-mindedness when he was home. It was obvious that she suspected him of having an affair. Let her think that! Far better than if she would catch on to the truth.

He became somber as he considered that the February fiasco was evidence that he had made a mistake with asking Member Six on board. Up until then, the group had been able to hold to their non-violence code. True, it was already the beginning of April now, and neither the police nor anyone else seemed to have an inkling of who was responsible for the Cubbyhole incident. There was a good chance that the crime would never be solved. Still, he was uneasy and realized he might come to regret his decision to go ahead with their next heist. Too late to change his mind now; things were already set in motion.

Chapter 12

R. A. Huber arrived first for her appointment with Yuri Novokoff at the Starbucks on North Hill Avenue. She ordered an espresso and found a seat at a small table for two. The place was moderately busy for late morning on a Tuesday. The majority of patrons consisted of young people with only their laptops for company, which came as no surprise to Huber since Pasadena City College was only a block away. Over the phone Mr. Novokoff had mentioned that he would be identifiable by wearing a beige scarf. As soon as she had hung up, she thought, did I understand correctly, a scarf? Indeed the weather had suddenly turned a bit chilly, but she couldn't remember the last time she had seen a man wearing a scarf in Southern California.

She noticed him as soon as he entered. He was middle aged, of medium height, and kept his light hair longish, covering part of a wide face. The silk scarf thrown over his shoulder trailed behind his brown suede jacket as he went straight to the counter to place his beverage order. Then he turned around, cappuccino in hand, and his eyes scanned the room. Huber got to her feet and signaled him over. When he stood next to her she introduced herself. His appearance may have been eccentric, but his manner was formal and impeccable.

He extended his hand and said, "Pleased to meet you, Ms. Huber," and waited until she sat back down before he grabbed his chair.

"I prefer Mrs." Then she inquired, "Are you from Russia?"

"Only second generation; Dad is Russian and Mom American. Why do you ask?"

"I'm just curious. Your name sounds Russian, but you don't have an accent."

"Accents can be simulated," and he suddenly became extremely Russian as he continued, "*Da, da,* is true my father vas a pianist and come to US to perform. He defected and never vent back to Soviet Union and I sure glad, otherwise never I be born."

Huber chuckled. "Am I right in assuming that you are not only an acting instructor, but a performer as well?"

"I've been in a few plays," he said modestly.

Then she got down to business and asked, "What can you tell me about Megan Maguire?"

"I wish I could help you with your investigation, but as I already told the police, I know nothing about what led to Megan's tragic death."

"Oh, I'm not suggesting that you do. I'm just trying to piece together what sort of a young woman she was. I understand that she attended a class in your theater department at PCC."

"Not just one class; Megan took three courses. The first was *Acting Fundamentals,* which is strictly a lecture course. It teaches principles of acting techniques, such as characterization interpretation, movement and voice. Next she enrolled in *Intermediate Acting,* which consists of some lecture, but mostly laboratory. It covers acting techniques for stage and camera, and teaches characterization through script and interpretation. The course is a solid preparation for performance. And last, she took *Advanced Acting Fundamentals,* again vastly laboratory with some lecture. It deals with application of performance technique and support activities for stage and camera productions, as well as advanced character development and study of period styles and genres."

He sighed and said, "Megan was in the process of taking the advanced course when she died."

"Was she a good student?"

"The best; one of few with real promise."

"Did you see her perform at the Cubbyhole Theater?"

A smile hushed over his broad face. "Yes, I was there. She 'lived' her role and I was extremely proud of her." And his expression turned to gloom when he added, "I heard the explosion as I walked to my car, but didn't know what had happened until the next day when I read it in the local paper."

Huber gave him a searching glance and asked, "Did you know Megan outside your capacity as her instructor?"

He paused before replying, "As I mentioned, Megan had promise. I took an interest in her future as an actress and she came to me for advice."

"What kind of advice?"

"I answered her numerous questions about whether to get an agent and join a union. I told her that she first needed to build a résumé. She knew that I had connections to the theater world and asked me if auditioning for a part with the amateur group was a good idea."

"And?"

"I planned to use my clout to help her get a start in the field as soon as she'd finished the advanced course. So I told her that meanwhile she would benefit from the experience and to go ahead with joining the amateur group. A play of the caliber of *From Sin to Virtue*, directed by none other than Sal Silverberg - - regardless that the man is retired and chips in out of the goodness of his heart - - would look impressive on her résumé." He sighed again and continued, "Now I know that my advice was her death sentence."

"Don't blame yourself, Mr. Novokoff. I imagine that the culprit would have found another way to kill Megan had she not performed in the play."

"Maybe, and maybe not; the murderer could be among the theater group."

"Yes, that has crossed my mind also."

Neither one spoke for a few moments, and then Huber asked, "Do you know any of the other performers of the *From Sin to Virtue* production?"

"No, I'd never met any of them before watching the play, and none had been my student."

"What did you think of them as actors?"

"They put on good performances; I was pleasantly surprised. In addition to Megan, who was superb, the woman who played Mother Earth also made a tremendous impression on me."

They had both long finished their coffees, and Yuri Novokoff looked at his watch and said, "I don't want to be rude, Mrs. Huber, but is that all the questions you had? I have to lecture in 15 minutes."

"By all means, I don't want to hold you up. Thank you for the interview."

He gave her a firm handshake and then she watched him taking brisk steps toward the exit with the scarf fluttering in his wake.

Chapter 13

The next person on Huber's list was Sal Silverberg, the director of the play. He owned a restaurant in Arcadia and had told her she could drop by anytime in the afternoon. When leaving the Starbucks coffee shop, she decided not to go back to her office and head for the City of Arcadia, since she was already well on her way. She drove along Colorado Boulevard for about five miles and then turned into Baldwin Avenue. Passing the Arboretum on her right, she got a glimpse of its fountain spurting ribbons of water high into the air. Across the street, a road led to the Santa Anita Race Track, one of the finest horse race parks in the country, and next to it, the Santa Anita Mall. At the Huntington Drive intersection Huber turned left and then passed by the Santa Anita golf Course.

Half a mile farther, she thought, I should be getting close now and had better check the street numbers. There was no need. She saw the big restaurant sign from a distance: *On Broadway*. She parked her car and checked the time. It was only 11:30 a.m. Might as well have an early lunch, she told herself, and entered. The place was not busy yet and after inquiring if she was lunching alone, the hostess escorted Huber to a small table and handed her a menu. All the dishes had names of celebrities. Before long, a waiter took her order of a Liza Minnelli, a Caesar salad.

While waiting for the food, Huber studied her surroundings. A kaleidoscope of photos with stage legends were displayed on the elongated parallel walls. She recognized the faces of Fred Astaire, Gregory Peck, Rex Harrison, Angela Lansbury, Olympia Dukakis, Cary Grant, and Lauren Bacall, to name a few. An old poster of

Stage Door depicting Ginger Rogers, Katherine Hepburn and Lucille Ball especially caught her eye. At the end of the room, next to the door leading into the kitchen, there was a floor-to-ceiling mural portraying nothing but hundreds of clapping hands. The effect was ingenious. No matter at which table one was seated throughout the restaurant, there was a strong feeling of being among stars that were applauded by an audience.

The Liza Minnelli was tasty and Huber savored every bite. By the time she had finished her meal, the lunch crowd arrived and *On Broadway* filled up rapidly. She took care of the bill and tip, but lingered on.

When the waiter came back to her table inquiring if he could bring her something else, she said, "I'm actually here to talk with Mr. Silverberg."

"Is there a problem?"

"Not at all, he's expecting me. I'm R. A. Huber."

"Oh sure, I'll get him."

Moments later, she came face to face with the director. He was angular, in his late sixties, had a curly white head of hair and a pair of piercing gray eyes behind wire-rimmed glasses. Clad in a button-down open-collar shirt, dark green trousers and a charcoal blazer, he gave the impression of a casual entrepreneur. Regardless of his laid-back demeanor, his persona radiated authority.

After introductions were made, Huber looked around the room and remarked, "This is clever. I'm impressed!"

"Thank you."

"The décor is all your own idea?"

"Sure, I'll take credit for that. Did you know that all these stars on the wall had their debut on Broadway?"

"I never thought about it," she replied.

"When I retired as Broadway director and moved west, I wanted to take a little of 'home' with me and opened this place."

"You're not the chef, I take it?"

"Good grief, no! I'd chase all the guests away with my cooking. I don't even run the place. My staff is savvy in the restaurant business and I'm wise enough not to interfere. I just show my face occasionally and mingle with the patrons. Some of my regulars are from the theater crowd and remember me."

"And you're still volunteering to direct plays, correct?"

"Old habits die hard," he replied with a grin. "I've taken on the jobs of director and stage manager all in one and enjoy working with the amateur group. There is less pressure and the performers are in it strictly for the love of acting."

Huber said, "That brings me to the reason I've come to talk with you. What was your professional evaluation of Megan Maguire?"

"Megan had talent. There's no question about that. She was a natural performer, and a fast study to boot. She never forgot a line, and to top it all was blessed with striking looks. In my opinion, she would have gone far. It's a pity that her life was taken before she had a chance to shine."

A couple passed by their table and the man said, "How's it going, Sal?"

Silverberg responded, "No complaints here. Nice to see you both again. I'll catch up with you later."

Then he turned back to Huber and continued, "I was so impressed with Megan that I begged Ralph Weatherford to come to opening night to see her perform."

"The famous theater critic?"

"The same."

"And did he come to see the play?"

"Yes, he was there."

"Was Megan well-liked by her peers?"

He thought about this for a moment and then answered, "Everyone appreciated her presence and talent on stage. I think the male actors admired her both in and out of the limelight. As for the ladies, there may have been some jealousies, here and there."

"Enough to want to inflict harm?"

"Certainly not," he protested.

"Were you in the theater at the time of the explosion?"

"Naturally, I watched the premiere. I was on my way backstage to congratulate everyone for a job well done, when all hell broke loose. When I got to the disastrous spot in the hallway, most actors were already there, gaping at the hole that used to be Megan's dressing room. Frantic, I called out to her, but there was no response and I suspected the worst. I called 911 right away and the police, fire department and paramedics arrived promptly. As I found out later, Megan was killed instantaneously, which at least was a blessing under the circumstances."

"I understand that the play has continued after the tragedy."

"I was shocked and saddened by Megan's murder, but 'the show must go on' is my motto. After all, plenty of tickets for future performances had been purchased. So Megan's understudy stepped up to the role of Vanity."

"My assistant and I would like to interview some of the actors. I know that they all have daytime jobs, so maybe we could talk with them briefly at the Cubbyhole. Do you think that's possible?"

"We have two weekend shows, Saturday and Sunday nights. The actors could be too pre-occupied before and too wound-up after their performance, but maybe Wednesday evening during rehearsal might work."

"That's tomorrow. Sounds good to me. May I also talk to the stagehand who accepted the orchid pot for Megan?"

"That would be Nancy. I'll make sure that she sticks around tomorrow night."

"I'm delighted to have your full cooperation."

"Believe me; I'm just as anxious to get the matter solved as you are. Some of the actors are edgy since the explosion and I don't want their performance influenced by apprehension. The police seem to be dragging their feet, so I have no choice but to put my faith in you."

Huber said, "We'll do our best." Then she thanked him and got up to leave while Mr. Silverberg went to chat with his patrons.

Chapter 14

On Wednesday morning, Huber sat at the computer in her office and looked over the Megan Maguire case notes she had written. Earlier at the gym, she had received her adrenaline fix. Nothing stimulated her body and mind more than a competitive racquet ball match. Drenched in sweat and in dire need of a shower, she had left the court with the knowledge that she could still give her opponent a good game. Considering that the man was ten years her junior, this was no small accomplishment.

Now she printed out her notes, reading the pages once more before adding them to the case folder. Huber enjoyed the freedom of the electronic age, but was old-fashioned enough to also keep paper records. She went over the rest of the data in the open folder spread before her and knew that sometime in the near future she would have to see Megan's parents in Portland, Oregon. Might as well not procrastinate and make a date now, she decided, and reached for the phone.

The instant she finished talking with Eileen Maguire and was in the process of posting the appointment on her calendar, the phone rang.

"Private investigating, R. A. Huber."

"How ya doin', Mrs. Huber? I handed in my last final and am now on spring break, ready to pitch in."

"Well, hello Andi. Something just occurred to me; did you have plans for spring break?"

"Kinda, but sleuthing comes first."

"Spoken like a true detective!"

"So who do I tackle?"

"You can set up an interview with Ralph Weatherford. His office is on the Westside, not far from where you live."

"I don't remember his name on Sergeant Wolf's list."

"He's not on it, and as far as I know, the police haven't questioned him. Sal Silverberg, the director, mentioned that Mr. Weatherford was in the audience that night. Maybe you don't know who he is."

"I haven't got a clue."

"Ralph Weatherford is a notable theater critic and reviewer."

"Holy Krewe! I get to interview a famous dude."

"I also want you to come to the Cubbyhole Theater tonight; we'll split up and talk to the actors during their rehearsal. I'll decide on the spur of the moment which are yours to question and which I'll take on."

"Sure thing, boss."

"If you like, you can sleep in our guest bedroom so you won't have to ride all the way home on your motorcycle late at night."

"That's mighty obligin' of you! I'll pack my touring bag."

"Do you have a pen handy?"

"Yes, ma'am."

"Okay, here is Ralph Weatherford's number and address," and she gave it to her. "I'll meet you at the Cubbyhole at seven o'clock."

Chapter 15

Sal Silverberg led the way to the green room where cast members were scattered about the place. Some were reading and rehearsing their lines, but most were standing around in small groups, chatting.

The director clapped his hands twice and obtained immediate silence. He said, "Attention, please!" and introduced the two women in his tow. "This is R. A. Huber and her assistant Antoinette LeJeune. They are private investigators hired to look into Megan's death. During this evening's rehearsal, they'll interview some of you when off stage. Please give them your undivided cooperation. Mrs. Huber will do her questioning in the storage room, and Ms. LeJeune has the dimmer room at her disposal."

He hollered, "Hey, Nancy!"

Out of nowhere a middle-aged woman appeared, presumably Nancy.

"Nancy will show you to the rooms, and may I suggest that you interview her first. She is our volunteer stagehand and I'd like to send her home afterwards. You can also question Todd; he's not needed at the moment."

Huber was about to thank him, but he had already turned his back on them and was busy instructing the actors what scenes he was going to drill them on first.

As they followed Nancy out of the green room, Todd Brighton disengaged himself from the group and did likewise.

The stagehand stopped by the dimmer room and turning to Andi said, "Here you are, Miss."

Huber glanced inside. Two folding chairs were set up in the small room amid dimmer racks. She said, "Andi, go ahead and interview Todd. I'll talk with Nancy."

Nancy had also provided folding chairs in the good-sized storage area piled with scenic elements, costume racks, sound equipment and the like.

Settled in, Huber said, "Thank you for making yourself available this evening."

The stagehand replied, "I don't mind."

"How long have you been volunteering here?"

"Five years."

"That's true dedication!"

"I love theater."

"Now I'd like you to go back in your mind to the debut night of the play. You accepted the orchid delivery for Megan Maguire. Correct?"

"That's right. They were fuchsia and light-pink."

"Who delivered them?"

"He said that he was from Champion Arrangements."

"And that wasn't the case?"

"I already told this to the police. At the time I had no idea that there isn't a florist by that name."

"Nobody faults you for that, I'm sure. You said 'he.' So it was a man who delivered the orchids?"

"I think so."

"You're not sure?"

"I guess it could've been a tall woman."

Huber was puzzled and said, "You didn't get a good look at the person who handed you the pot of flowers?"

"Right."

This is like pulling teeth, Huber thought. She then asked, "What was the person wearing?"

"Jeans and a hooded sweat jacket."

"I'm starting to understand. Was the hood pulled down over the face, covering most of it?"

"Yes."

"What was the person's body build?"

"Tall and lanky, like most kids that age."

"So you know the person's age?"

"Of course not! I just figured him being a young guy by the way he was dressed. Most kids walk around in awful clothes nowadays, with holes in their jeans and tops three sizes too large for them, not to mention tattoos all over their bodies."

Amused, Huber felt that this was the longest speech the lady was capable of giving. And she continued, "What kind of a voice did he have?"

"Not deep and not high-pitched either."

"Any accent?"

"I don't think so."

"You're not certain?"

"He only said a few words: 'Delivery for Megan Maguire from Champion Arrangements.'"

"So you took the orchids from him and what did you do next?"

"Carried them to Megan's dressing room and set them down on her table."

"Now Nancy, this is extremely important; did you get side-tracked for some reason on your way to Megan's dressing room and leave the pot of orchids sitting somewhere else for a few moments?"

"No, I took it straight to her dressing room and placed it on the table."

"Was anyone there?"

"No, the room was empty."

"When was the delivery made?"

"I didn't look at my watch."

"I meant, during what segment of the play?"

"Oh, that I know for a fact. It was during the last act and close to final curtain."

Huber said, "You do realize that it is possible a theater group member is responsible for Megan's murder."

Nancy shook her head.

"You don't agree that it's a possibility?"

"No," she stated, "we are good people."

"It's that simple for you. I hope you are right," Huber replied.

Chapter 16

In the dimmer room Andi and Todd sat in their folding chairs, facing one another. Andi had already noticed that he was tall and handsome - - and that he knew it - - as they walked over from the green room. Now she studied his features at close range. The thirty-seven-year old man sported dark medium-long hair sleeked back and parted on the side, and a pair of black intense eyes. Andi glanced at the information sheet Mrs. Huber had supplied her with.

She said, "You're Todd Brighton?"

"Guilty as charged," he replied, his dark eyes full of mischief.

"I see that you are married, have two kids, and work as a store manager."

"And here I was going to keep all that a secret from you!"

Andi ignored the remark and asked, "Why did you join an amateur theater group?"

"Because acting is my true calling." And with a mocking gesture he went on, "The rest of my life is camouflage."

"Which *From Sin to Virtue* character are you?"

"I play Pride, which is equal with the devil."

"You look the part; all that's missin' are the horns."

"I put those on at each performance."

And before she had a chance to properly run the interview, he asked "How does someone like you become a private investigator?"

"I hit the jackpot."

"Oh that's how it's done!" Then he said, "That employer of yours, isn't she rather old for the job?"

Andi shot back, "She's no spring chicken, but nobody better mess with Mrs. Huber. She's sharp as a spike and sleuthing comes naturally. As for physical stamina, I reckon she'd give you a lickin' at racquet ball any day of the week, and she's a dang good shot, which, if you're lucky, you won't have to find out for yourself."

"Sorry if I've offended you."

"Now let's get to it. Tell me about Megan Maguire."

"If you mean why she was murdered, I have no idea. She didn't confide in me."

"Did you like working with her?"

"She was a gifted actor and I respected her as such. We had good chemistry on stage. As for off stage, she didn't give me the time of day."

"Did that bother you?"

He gave her an arrogant stare from his black eyes and replied, "I'm not used to getting snubbed."

"Was Megan behaving differently before and during her performance on that fatal night?"

"Not that I'd noticed."

Andi's glance roamed to the dimmer racks, her only other choice of view in the room besides Todd. Then her eyes focused on him again and she said, "I'd like to get a feeling of where everyone was, shortly before, at the moment, and right after the explosion. So fill me in."

He thought about it for a second and then said, "At the last scene, Megan had the stage to herself. The rest of us waited in the green room until she came to her last line and the curtain fell. That was our cue to hurry on stage and line up, before it rose again, to take our curtain call bows. A minute or so later, we all hurried to the lobby to mingle with the audience. Then we went to our respective dressing rooms."

"How many dressing rooms are there?"

"Oh, there's just one giant one for the ladies and another for the men. Megan was the only lucky person who was given her own private little room. Or should I say, unlucky as it turned out."

"Go on, please."

"I was getting out of my costume and was about to take off the stage make-up, when the big bang shook the entire building. At first, everyone froze. I heard some women scream, knowing that the outcries were coming from their dressing room. Then everyone ran out into the hallway to see what had happened. We all stopped short where part of the hallway and Megan's dressing room used to be. After the dust settled, there was nothing but a big hole with caved-in walls and a chaos of debris under which we assumed Megan lay buried."

He took a deep breath and continued, "It was a God-awful sight. Mr. Silverberg stood suddenly next to me and called Megan's name, but there was no movement below. Then he held everyone back, telling us not to touch anything. He called 911 and I believe most people were still in shock when we heard the sirens."

Neither spoke for some time, each preoccupied with their own thoughts. Todd found it hard to shake the scene from his memory and Andi, for her part, could well picture it as told in detail by him.

Then she asked, "How is the new Vanity working out?"

Todd replied, "Adriana was Megan's understudy and knows the lines, but she doesn't come close to Megan's caliber, nor has she the Vanity look."

He winked at her and said in his devilish Pride voice, "You, my pet, would be perfect with your cat-green eyes and fiery disposition. And the Southern drawl would lend an interesting flavor to the role. I'd love to perform with you." He playfully touched a strand of Andi's hair and added, "These flames of fire alone would light up the stage! Seriously, you should try out for the part."

Andi pulled away from his reach and stated, "I have no interest in acting."

"Our loss!"

"We're done with the interview. Thanks, Mr. Brighton."

Chapter 17

Mercedes Cleveland walked into the storage room with an agile gait. She was twenty-six, a single mom with two small children, African American, slender, quick-witted, and possessed a dry sense of humor. Huber had previously studied the theater program and knew which roles the main characters played.

She now motioned Mercedes into the folding chair opposite from hers and said, "You are Mother Earth in the play, correct?"

"Yeah, that's me."

"I picture that particular character as being older and a lot larger than you are."

Mercedes let out a roaring guffaw and replied, "You'd be surprised what a wig, make-up, and stuffing under the skirt can do for you!"

Huber couldn't help but burst into laughter herself.

The young woman continued, "I love the stage so much, I'll take any role that comes my way, big or small."

"What is your daytime job?"

"I work in a jewelry store."

"It must be hard to juggle work, kids, and your theater group."

"I manage and don't want to give any of it up. Work is for survival, the kids are my life, and acting is good for my soul."

"Well put! Now let me start my inquiry. What can you tell me about Megan Maguire?"

"Depends on what you want to know."

"Anything you'd like to contribute. How well you knew her, whether you got along, what kind of a person and actress she was. Those are the things I'd like to discover."

"I only knew her as part of the theater group; we didn't socialize outside of it. She was a natural and I loved to share the stage with her. She used perfect timing with her dialogue, always paid attention to her entrance and exit cues, and never forgot her lines. There was passion in her performance which was contagious, and so she made the rest of us look good. I'm sure I speak for the entire group when I tell you that Megan is greatly missed."

She paused and then said, "As for her person, I liked her fine, but didn't get to know her well. She was reserved."

"Several people told me that Megan had talent, but your description of her as a performer makes it real for me."

"A great many of us in the group are gifted, but we are amateurs and do our acting for the sheer pleasure of it." She did another of her belly laughs and continued, "In other words, it is an outlet from our everyday dreary lives. Megan was different. For her, this was just a stepping stone for greater things to come. If she'd lived, she'd have made a career of it."

"Did she appear different or worried lately?"

Mercedes took her time before she answered, "No, she seemed her usual self. She did jump, though, when I came to her dressing room to borrow a nail file. I shrugged it off as her having a case of nerves. After all, it was opening night."

"When was this?"

"During intermission."

"Did you notice what was on her table?"

"Not particularly. Let me think - - I remember a hairdryer and a book, but I don't recall the title."

"You didn't see any flowers; fuchsia and light-pink orchids, to be exact?"

"No, I surely would've noticed orchids had there been any."

"Did Megan make enemies among the cast?"

"There was a little cattiness going around. Some of the women begrudged her the lead role, but I wouldn't call them enemies."

"Do you have a theory of why someone wished her harm?"

"No, and believe me, I've thought long and hard about it ever since she was murdered. I don't think you should look for the killer among the theater group. Megan had a life outside the Cubbyhole stage."

"You have a point there. I'll keep it in mind."

Then Huber asked, "What do you think of the young woman, Adriana Rippling, who has taken over Megan's part?"

"She's okay, but can't hold a candle to Megan's acting." Then she let loose that spontaneous, carefree chuckle and added, "If she'd ask the mirror on the wall, 'Who's the cattiest in the land?' the mirror's response would be, 'You are, dear Adriana'!"

That concluded the interview.

As Mercedes walked toward the door, Huber called after her, "One more thing!"

She turned her head and said, "Yes?"

"That forcible laugh of yours; do you ever use it on stage?"

"It comes in handy at times!"

Chapter 18

Meanwhile, Andi interviewed Adriana Rippling. Andi had studied up on the woman beforehand. She was twenty-five, a wedding coordinator, single, and now played the role of Vanity.

Adriana walked into the dimmer room, lifted her chin, flipped her long brown hair, and stated, "It's claustrophobic in here. I hope this won't take long."

Andi gave her a brief look-over and decided that the woman would be pretty but for a permanent frown stamped onto her face. "I'll try not to waste much of your precious time."

Adriana rolled her brown eyes.

"Okay, have a seat and let's get started. Betcha being a wedding coordinator is a fun job."

"It is, most of the time. I've met some interesting people along the way and arranged quite a few marriage ceremonies and receptions for the rich and famous. I've organized so many weddings that once I tie the knot myself, I plan to chuck it all and just elope."

Getting on with business, Andi said, "I see that you stepped into Megan's shoes; how do they fit so far?"

Although there was less than four years difference between the two young women, Adriana thought, how dare this kid poke fun at me. Aloud she said, "They fit great, thank you! Actually, the part should have been mine to begin with."

"No jivin'?"

"I've been a member of the theater group for a long time and have seniority. I tried out for the part of Vanity and practically had it in my pocket when Megan showed up and stole it out from under my nose!"

"And that made you madder than a hatter?"

"Sure. Wouldn't you feel the same?"

"I reckon so."

Adriana suddenly eyed her keenly and then asked, "You're not after the part yourself, or are you?"

"Holy Krewe! Does everybody 'round here think I'm interested in acting?"

"Holy what?"

"A Krewe is an organization that parades at Mardi Gras. But never mind that, I'm not seekin' your Vanity character or any other role." She smiled and continued, "Now that we've got that settled, describe Megan to me please."

Adriana pursed her lips and said, "She had great looks and was talented, I give her that."

"But?"

"I didn't like her. I know one isn't supposed to speak ill of the dead, but I don't want to be a hypocrite. Everyone made a big deal over her - - Megan is so gifted - - Megan is incredibly beautiful - - Megan this and Megan that! Even our director treated her as his favorite. No wonder she was full of herself."

"She was mean to you?"

"Well, not exactly mean. Condescending is more like it."

"Gotcha."

Then Andi asked, "Were you here on Megan's disastrous night?"

"Sure, I wouldn't miss the premiere."

"Tell me what happened."

"I was in the audience; eighth row. You'd think that sitting through many rehearsals the way I did, the actual opening of the play would leave me cold, but not so. I was spellbound. Everybody gave a great performance, and Megan was brilliant, I had to admit. After final curtain, I got to my feet and cheered with the crowd. While the cast members mingled with theater goers in the lobby, I didn't want to take up their time, but stayed in my seat and waited. I was headed backstage to congratulate everybody when the blast hit and made the entire place shake. At first I was stunned and couldn't move. Then I started running and soon joined people rushing out of their dressing rooms and followed them into the hallway. We came to a stop in front of a deep pit, all in shambles, where Megan's dressing room used to be. It was horrible. I knew right away that any breath of life would be impossible underneath that rubble."

She shivered and there was true emotion in her eyes when she said, "I had wished on several occasions that Megan would drop dead, but now that it was a fact, I felt nothing but shock and sadness."

Andi did not say a word, but looked at her steadily.

"Oh my God! You don't think I had anything to do with the explosion, do you? Wanting her out of the way was just wishful thinking, I swear!"

"Who do you think had a real motive for killing Megan?"

"I have no idea, honest. It might have been an accident."

"A bomb going off seems accidental to you?"

"What I meant is, whoever did it screwed up. The person may be a maniac who has a grudge against the owners of the Cubbyhole, or maybe the director, or he could even have a problem with the play itself. You know, a religious fanatic, or some other nut. I imagine he just wanted to cause a scene and shake everybody up. He may have thought that the entire cast was still in the lobby and that nobody was in Megan's dressing room or in the hallway."

Andi remarked, "That sure is a different way of looking at things." Then she checked her watch and exclaimed, "I plumb forgot promising to keep our talk short, and here I've been hangin' onto you for 15 minutes!"

Chapter 19

The private investigators each talked to several other theater group members, but learned little more. The general sentiment among the cast was that Megan Maguire had been admired for her acting, but had not been an easy person to get to know personally. They had all rushed to the horrendous site after the explosion and were appalled by what they saw. Many feared that if the perpetrator was a nutcase holding a grudge against actors, his crime would not stop with Megan and that he might attack others at any moment.

When Huber and Andi suggested that a member of their acting group was most likely the culprit, they seemed shocked and full of protest. They admitted that there was a bit of rivalry going down among the performers, but nothing more serious than that. The idea that one of their own could resort to such violence was rejected by all.

It was getting late in the evening and there was only one person left to interview. Huber asked Andi to join her in the storage room for the questioning of Chad Lindhurst. Their record of him showed the following: 41 years old, electronics technician, divorced, and cast as the character Fortitude in the play.

He came into the room with a diffident manner, contrary to most of the other actors who had clearly made an entrance. He was tall, of pale complexion, had blue eyes, a chiseled nose, a narrow face, and blond hair.

He said, "Mr. Silverberg excused me for the night, so I'm all yours." His voice matched his demeanor. It was soft, low, and precise.

Huber said, "You must be anxious to go home so we'll try not to prolong our talk. How long have you been with the theater group?"

"Three years."

"Does it give you a creative outlet that's missing from your technician job?"

"I never thought of it that way." He grinned sheepishly and went on, "At the time, my girlfriend practically forced me to join the group."

"Would that be Madame Dubois?"

Surprised, he replied, "I see you've talked to her and she's not keeping our relationship a secret."

Huber asked, "What did you mean by her forcing you?"

"Well, I was kind of antisocial and Annette - - that's Madame Dubois - - insisted that being part of an acting group would help me with my problem."

"You are shy?"

"Not precisely." He hesitated for a second and then said, "Oh hell, I might as well spill my guts. The truth is, after I came back from serving in the Gulf War, I was a changed man. Among other things, I left a dead comrade behind. That was Annette's husband, by the way. After coming home, I had a heck of a time. One day my wife left me, because I'd become impossible to live with. After many years of being down in the dumps, Annette took a chance on me, and I think I'm finally managing to lead a normal life."

He suddenly was embarrassed and said "I've no idea why I told you all this."

Huber said, "Acting seems to do the trick; you've stuck with it for three years."

"I've come to enjoy it," he admitted.

"Are you considering making a career of it?"

"No, I like the amateur setting. We are extremely lucky that Sal Silverberg took an interest in our current play and volunteered to direct it. As you can imagine, that's not the norm in our theater group."

"Who directs the plays as a rule?"

"All of us. We take turns filling the jobs of director and stage manager. He smiled and added, "I never mind the experience when the position is dealt out to me. Looking at a play from the director's angle is different from that of the actor's."

"You get to wear different hats."

"Absolutely, we even create our own scenery. On weekends before the premiere, you can see us cutting, hammering, gluing, and painting wood or cardboard in the parking lot."

Huber remarked, "I can see that an amateur production has a charm of its own. Then she got to her objective and said, "What can you tell us about Megan?"

"I suppose you've learned already from everyone else that she was talented, so I won't dwell on that. The stage was in fact her whole life. Off stage, she was just a homesick kid."

"She confided in you?"

"We went out on a few dates."

"I see."

"Nothing serious. As I said, she was a kid. Many guys in our group asked her out, but she was picky. I'll admit, it flattered my ego to be one of the chosen few."

"Did Megan seem frightened lately?"

"Not to my knowledge."

"Do you have any idea who could have wanted to harm her?"

"There were some jealousies among the females in our group, but the only one who seemed to truly hate her was

Adriana. And, frankly, I can't picture Adriana placing a bomb in Megan's dressing room."

"Where were you when it went off?"

"I was in the men's dressing room just about to take off my costume."

"Do you remember who else was there?"

"I didn't pay much attention, but I assume all the other male actors were changing too."

"That's all, thank you." She turned to her assistant and asked, "How about it, Andi? Do you have any questions for Mr. Lindhurst?"

"Just one. How did your dating Megan sit with Madame Dubois?"

He grinned and replied, "I didn't tell her, and unless either one of you ladies let the cat out of the bag, she'll never know."

After he left, Huber walked to a curtain drawn against the wall of the storage room and peeked behind it. She discovered rows of shelves housing props and the like. She looked at Andi and said, "There's plenty of space here for hiding something."

"What's on your mind, boss?"

"I was thinking of an orchid pot."

Chapter 20

Andi enjoyed a leisurely breakfast at the Huber residence. Then her boss poured her a second cup of coffee and said, "Let's go over last night's interviews."

Peter got to his feet and declared, "I'll leave you sleuths to your homework," and left the kitchen.

So Huber and Andi had their powwow, clueing one another in on the questioning of the suspects. Besides giving an account of the conversations, they also related the impression each person had made on them.

About Todd Brighton, Andi commented, "He's a womanizer, and being married with kids doesn't seem to stop him any. He was miffed when his charms and flattery didn't work on me. I reckon he didn't get anywhere with Megan either."

Huber asked, "And what did you make of Adriana Rippling?"

"There's cattiness about her. She even considered me as competition in her acting career. To her credit, she was honest about disliking Megan, and I believed her when she told me that wanting her dead was only wishful thinking."

"Keep in mind though, we're dealing with actors. They're good at disguising their true feelings."

"Sure thing, boss."

Huber said, "Mercedes Cleveland was refreshing to talk with and she appears to have a true love for the stage. She also has an earsplitting laugh that shocked the socks off me when I first heard it. Through her narrative, I hit upon Megan's acting persona. But what is essential to our investigation is the fact that she made Megan jump when coming into the dressing room to borrow a nail file. That's an indication that Megan was afraid of something or someone."

"You betcha!"

"As to Nancy, the stagehand," Huber commented, "in her opinion the theater group is 'good people' and no one in it could possibly have anything to do with Megan's murder. And our job would be too easy had the woman been able to give an exact description of the orchid delivery person."

"I think that's not all that important."

"You're right. The killer could have paid someone off the street to make the delivery, in which case a description would have been useless to us. Or, should the villain be among the performers, he or she could have easily slipped away at the crucial time, put on a hooded jacket, and handed Nancy the lethal orchid pot at the back door. She said that the person was tall, but considering her own petite size, anyone over 5'5" might seem tall to her."

"What crucial time?"

"Remember, Nancy gave us an approximate time frame. She mentioned that the delivery was made during the last act, which confirms what I learned from Mercedes, namely that at intermission there were no orchids in Megan's dressing room. And don't forget, Megan had the entire stage to herself towards the end of the play."

"Meaning any of the other actors could've handed over the flowers."

"Exactly."

Then she asked, "What was your impression of Chad Lindhurst?"

Andi grinned and said, "Megan seemed to have enjoyed his company."

"What else?"

"Well, I wonder if he's as meek as he comes across."

Huber nodded. "He appeared as tame as his character role. I found it interesting that he tagged Megan as a homesick kid. So far, we've found nobody here in California who was close to the young woman. I hope to get a better idea of what she was like when I see her parents."

"Explain something to me, boss. What did you have in mind when you looked at the shelves in the storage room and said that the orchid pot could've been hidden there?"

"Think about it: if one of the actors brought the pot with the bomb to the theater that evening, it needed to be hidden until the time was right."

"I still don't get it."

"Let's say the perpetrator arrived at the Cubbyhole before the play carrying a big shopping bag or a backpack. He - - it could have been a 'she', but I'll use 'he' for convenience - - sneaked into the storage room and hid the bag which contained a pair of jeans, a hooded jacket, and the orchid pot. Then he went about his acting business as usual. He got his chance during the final act when the cast - - except for Megan, who was on stage - - gathered in the green room waiting until final curtain to take a bow. He pretended to go to the restroom, but headed for the storage room instead, where he quickly changed. Moments later he turned up at the back door, telling Nancy that he had a delivery for Megan from Champion Arrangements. As soon as the coast was clear, he returned to the storage room and changed back into his costume. I imagine that later, when everyone was in an uproar about the explosion, he could have easily retrieved the shopping bag now only holding his clothes."

"Holy Krewe, I can picture it all! If he timed it right, it could all be done without much risk of being discovered."

Huber smiled and said, "It's all speculation, and for all we know the murderer might not be among the cast of actors at all."

Before Andi left she said, "By the way, I can't get a hold of the theater critic guy."

"Ralph Weatherford?"

"Uh-huh. I left voice mail messages, but he hasn't called back."

"Keep trying. Also, I'd like you to interview Brent Halifax, Megan's old boyfriend. He lives and works closer to your neck of the woods. You'll find information about him on your copy of the paperwork I received from Sergeant Wolf."

"Yes, ma'am."

Chapter 21

Huber found Peter in the family room.

She said, "Want to join me on a trip?"

Peter tore himself away from his laptop and asked, "To Portland, Oregon?"

"You *are* quick! Yes, that's where I'm headed."

"When?"

"My appointment with the Maguires is on Monday. I was going to fly, but if you come along, we could drive up and make a bit of a vacation out of it. I checked the forecast; fair weather is predicted up north over the next several days."

"Today is Thursday already."

"I was thinking we'd leave tomorrow."

"You sure give a fellow much notice! How long would we be gone?"

"About a week, give or take a day."

"Let me check." He went to get his appointment ledger and then stated, "I could manage it as long as the trip won't take longer than seven days. I have a book signing a week from Saturday."

"Don't worry, we'll be back in plenty of time," she assured him.

"In that case I could make myself available."

"Okay, that's settled then." She stepped closer and giving him a big hug declared, "You're such a good sport!"

Then she hurried out of the den and murmured, "I'd best get on the ball. I've got laundry to do, plants to water, dust and vacuum, pack our suitcase, and all that jazz."

Chapter 22

At 7:15 that evening, Member One was parked at the curb on a street in San Marino, keeping his eyes on a residence three houses away. A while ago, he had seen the housekeeper leave for her maid's night out. And if all went on schedule, the lady and gent of the mansion would soon drive to their bridge club meeting as they did every Thursday night. The research and blueprint for this particular job was complete, and he waited patiently to put his game plan into action.

He had an excellent team of experts. Among them there was a member who knew all about gems and precious metals. Another's mastery was in works of art. A former gymnast proved to be a wizard with ropes, and yet another member had great connections and a knack at extracting valuable tips from the rich and famous. There was a safe cracker and explosives expert. And last, an import/export entrepreneur who often traveled out of the country. Member One himself, as vice president of a bank, had access to the financial records of his potential victims, giving him an approximate idea of their worth. His partners in crime knew what he expected of them, but he was always present at each heist to orchestrate the show.

"There they go," he murmured as the garage door of the house opened, and a white newer model Cadillac CTS-V Sedan emerged, its headlights already turned on in the twilight of the evening. Member One crouched low in his seat when the car went by him but nonetheless identified the driver and passenger as the man and lady of the house, according to a photograph he had studied earlier.

Always immediately before a job, the anticipation of the thrill and risk involved excited him while at the same time his mind functioned like clockwork. He reached for his iPhone and connected to the internet. Once he logged on to his Yahoo group, he entered only two words: *green light*. Within moments, Members Two through Seven checked their Yahoo group e-mail and got the *green light* confirmation to proceed.

An hour later, dusk had turned into night with only a street light many yards away to break the darkness. The members were on the spot and ready to proceed. Their leader signaled to Member Four, the acrobat, who was on top of the concrete wall in no time. In order to bypass the alarm sensors on the ground, he leaped onto the nearest tree to the house from where he swung from branch to branch like a monkey until he reached the top of the mansion. Once on the roof, disabling the entire burglar alarm by cutting the phone line was easy. Then he lowered himself to an unlocked second story window and let himself in through it.

Moments later, he opened the front door from inside to let the rest of the gang in, except for Member Seven who stayed in his parked car across the street as lookout. Member One directed traffic, so to speak. He motioned Member Six to head to the master bedroom upstairs where the safe was located. The rest methodically scanned each room for valuables, first downstairs and then on the second floor. Member Three scrutinized pictures on the walls. Most proved to be prints with no great value. He got excited when he came upon an original watercolor landscape in the living room. The painting was relatively small, 12" x 16", including the frame. On close examination, he determined that the watercolor was indeed by Woodward. He carefully took it off the wall and placed it near the front door. In the dining room's china cabinet, he spotted an 8" multi-tone Tiffany Favrile glass vase as well as several rare Lladro figurines. He brought the items to the front entrance hall, where Member Five took the precious objects from him and wrapped them in bubble plastic sheeting, one by one.

Gem expert Member Two had been sifting through a jewelry case on the dresser in the master bedroom while Member Six was busy cracking the safe. The case was loaded with gold and silver hoop earrings, custom necklaces, bangles, pendants and the like, but although good quality, nothing was of substantial value. A tennis bracelet had the look of diamonds, but on closer scrutiny turned out to be made from cubic zirconia.

Member One entered the master bedroom and asked the safe cracker, "How's it going?"

Continuing with his task, and without looking away or being deterred from his objective, Member Six answered, "I'm done with the weak-point drilling." And while observing the lock, he manipulated the dial to align the lock gates. Moments later the fence fell and the bolt was disengaged.

"Good job!" said Member One as he reached inside the safe.

The bottom compartment was stacked with documents, such as the deed to the house, passports, pink slips for cars, stocks and bonds, etcetera. Member One did not touch any of these items and went straight for the ornate antique jewelry box that sat on the top shelf. He opened it, glanced inside, and then passed it on to the expert, who studied each jewelry piece under a magnifier. There were white and yellow gold necklaces and bracelets, mostly 14-karat with a couple of 18-karat chains thrown in for good measure. Gems of a variety of color and shape came to light. An antique radiant ruby and diamond ring with matching pendant especially caught Member Two's eye as she laid the pieces out on the dresser for evaluation. A small cry of joy escaped her when she happened upon an exquisite Colombian emerald and diamond set. It consisted of a necklace, drop earrings, and a ring cast in platinum.

She weighed each item in her hands appreciatively and announced, "This is a unique find!"

Member One gathered all the jewels and took a quick inventory, listing the pieces on his   iPad before dropping them into a good-sized velvet pouch. Then he returned the empty jewelry case to the safe and said, "Let's get out of here."

Downstairs, he handed the pouch to Member Five for temporary safekeeping while its content was "hot."

"Oh, we're ready to leave? Just a second!" Member Five cackled and ran up the stairs. Member One frowned in disapproval. He considered his jobs serious business and expected his crew to respect them as such.

On the second floor Member Five placed a toy monkey hanging by its tail from the master bedroom lamp and then descended the staircase still laughing.

There had been no texting from Member Seven warning about anyone approaching the property or suspicious neighbors, so their leader opened the front door and peeked out with caution to make sure that the coast was clear. Then six dark shadows slipped out of the mansion and the grounds. The watercolor, Tiffany vase, and Lladro figurines were stored in the trunk of Member Seven's car parked across the street, while Member Five was left in temporary custody of the jewels. Everyone walked to their respective vehicles - - parked a short distance away on side streets - - removed their masks, and drove out of the neighborhood.

The entire heist had only taken about an hour.

Chapter 23

The Hubers had a late start taking off on Friday morning. What with last minute household chores, tossing toilet essentials into a bag, and asking their next door neighbor to take in their mail for a week, it was nearly ten o'clock when they left their Merida residence.

Peter took the wheel of the SUV for the first leg of the journey and before they reached the end of the block he said, "I didn't even have time to read the paper."

Regula asked, "You've packed your laptop?"

"I wouldn't leave home without it!"

"There you go; tonight you can read the local newspaper online."

The drive north on Interstate 5 was a boring choice, but by far the fastest way to get to the Oregon border. There was still a chain of wild flowers in plain view on the hillside near Gorman and over the Grapevine, although the hot summer months ahead would soon erase any trace of the splendid flora.

Peter asked, "Did you let the kids know about this trip?"

"Sure. I called them both. Ben said, 'Have fun and good hunting,' but Deborah didn't take it so lightly."

"You told her the purpose of our journey?"

"Reluctantly, but she left me no choice short of lying. She wanted to know the reason for this spur-of-the-moment trip."

Peter grinned and said, "I can imagine our Sunshine's reaction," and he mimicked their daughter's hi-pitched voice as he exclaimed, "'So you're still chasing criminals and putting yourself in danger. At your age, that's a crime in itself, in my opinion! Mom, don't you think it's high time you gave up that investigating business of yours? I can't see what you're trying to prove! And Dad seems to be condoning your irresponsibility by playing along.'"

"Close enough. You do her so well, Peter! She also wanted us to stop by their place, but I told her that there's no time for a detour on our way up. I left it open whether we'll drive down the coast and pay them a short visit on the way home."

To keep Peter alert during the monotonous long stretch on I-5, Regula chose a rock CD mix from - Scorpions – Journey – Queen – Elton John - Rod Stewart - to listen to. Halfway between L. A. and Sacramento they smelled the Harris Ranch cattle long before they saw the herd.   The couple took a lunch break and made two more pit stops at rest areas to stretch and use the bathrooms. By five o'clock they drove through Sacramento and checked in at a Holiday Inn Express at the outskirts of town.

Returning to their hotel room from an enjoyable dinner at a nearby sports bar and a stroll through the neighborhood, Peter pulled out his laptop, connected to the Internet, and finally got around to reading his paper while Regula buried her head in a novel.

She was comfortably immersed in her story when her spouse suddenly said, "The monkey tail burglar has been at it again!"

It took her a moment to fully catch on to what he was talking about, and then she asked, "Where and when?"

"He broke into a mansion in San Marino last night and got away with a loot of over $200,000. The jewelry alone was insured for $130,000."

Regula slid her bookmark into the current page and put the book aside, giving Peter her full attention. She said, "Why would anyone leave that kind of jewelry sitting around?"

"The gems were kept in a safe, which he was able to crack."

"These burglaries have been going on way too long without the police catching on. The guy seems to be a wizard."

Peter said, "I believe that the heists have been planned and executed by a well organized group of thieves. One guy cannot possibly be an expert in disabling burglar alarms, cracking safes, and be savvy about art and jewelry in order to know precisely which items to steal. Also, there must be inside connections to know which houses and people to target."

"I can see that you've been giving this a lot of thought."

He tapped the laptop screen with his index finger and said, "Yes, this monkey business intrigues me."

Chapter 24

On Friday evening, Andi entered the establishment where Brent Halifax worked as a bartender. Although Daddy's old-fashioned bar in New Orleans could have never compared with this high-end place on the Westside of the Los Angeles area, she felt an instant connection of "coming home" as she entered. The time was only eight o'clock. and the bar was not yet in full swing. A few patrons were scattered at small tables, and about six guys sat at the bar, watching a Lakers basketball game on a big-screen TV. Andi hoisted herself onto a barstool.

She knew from Sergeant Wolf's notes that the bartender in front of her was 25 years old, had migrated to California approximately two years ago, and had lost his folks in a car crash when in his last year of high school. Not in the notes was the fact that he had a full head of curly dark hair, light eyes, and was ruggedly attractive.

He said, "Your I.D. please."

Andi showed it to him, and he asked, "What can I do for you, Antoinette LeJeune?"

"How 'bout fixing a Ramos Fizz?"

"You mean a New Orleans Fizz?"

"Same thing!"

"Sure, I'm equipped to throw that together for you."

Andi paid close attention as he placed gin, lime and lemon juice, simple syrup, half and half cream, egg white and fleurs d'orange into a cocktail shaker with ice cubes. Then he shook it vigorously, making sure the egg and cream were well mixed. Finally he strained it all into a highball glass filled with ice and then topped it off with club soda. She had watched Daddy numerous times fixing a Ramos Fizz and on rare occasions he had let her have a sip or two, even though she was not of legal drinking age at the time.

He said, "Voilà, your whatever fizz," and placed the cocktail in front of her.

Andi tasted it and announced, "Perfect!" Then she gave him a direct glance and said, "Am I lookin' at Brent Halifax?"

"Yeah, how did you know, foxy Antoinette?"

"I go by Andi and work for R. A. Huber, Private Investigating."

"No kidding!"

"Mr. and Mrs. Maguire hired us to investigate the murder of their daughter, Megan Maguire."

All the light-hearted banter suddenly went out of him as he said, "I don't know anything about it. I cooperated with the police but don't have to talk to you. So I suggest you finish your drink and leave."

"Don't you want the killer caught?"

"Of course I do. But you can't pin this on me. I had nothing to do with it. And for your information, I'm not the least bit handy with explosives."

"I wasn't making an accusation."

He calmed down and remarked, "It's always easy to target an ex-boyfriend as the villain."

"You have a point there, but under the circumstances you can't blame the police or my investigating firm to look into the matter."

"What circumstances?"

"You followed Megan from Portland to California."

"Who said I did?"

"It's listed in the information we gathered."

"Megan's mother probably made that up. The woman never liked me. Anyway, that's crap; I came to California to make a better living."

"Sorry, my mistake."

Andi took a couple of swigs from her Ramos Fizz and mulled over how best to proceed when a man seated a couple of stools down the bar scooted over to her, saying, "Can I buy you a drink, honey?"

"I'm buying my own, thank you."

"Has anyone told you that you're a looker?"

The man was obviously no longer sober and Brent said, "Leave her alone, she's with me."

The man went back to his stool, murmuring, "I thought that chicks were public domain in a bar."

Andi said, "Where were we? Oh yeah - - your move to Southern California. How do you like it here?"

"Can't complain."

"So you enjoy bartending?"

He shot her an angry glance and stated, "I would've preferred a college education, but had to support myself since I was eighteen."

"You've lost your parents?"

He nodded.

"We have something in common then. My folks died also."

He seemed to warm up to her a little and remarked, "Then you know how it is."

"You betcha." Then she said, "Tell me about Megan."

"What about her?"

"How long did you date?"

"For a year or so when we both lived in Portland."

"Who broke up?"

"It was mutual. She didn't want the kind of relationship I had in mind, so we called it quits."

"Meaning she didn't commit?"

"You got it."

"What did you mean earlier when you mentioned that her momma never liked you?"

"I wasn't good enough for her precious Megan."

He seemed to realize how nasty that sounded and added, "Megan's parents were overprotective of her to the point of ridiculous."

"In what way?"

"Megan and I once took a weekend trip to San Francisco together and they suggested a chaperon. We're in the 21st century, for crying out loud!"

"Did Megan drop out of college before or after the two of you broke up?"

"Soon after, I think."

"Do you know why she came to California?"

"That's easy; her main reason was that she wanted to become an actress. As a matter of fact, she was obsessed with the idea. Where else would she have a better chance of achieving her goal than right here?"

"So who came down first?"

"She did. I moved a couple of months later."

The guys at the bar cheered the Lakers on as the ballgame neared the last few minutes. Momentarily distracted, Andi looked up at the TV screen and Brent moved to the other end of the bar to refill his customer's drinks.

Then they picked up the conversation again and Andi asked, "You did hook up with Megan, though, when you got to California, right?"

"True."

"How did you find her?"

"Her best friend gave me her address before I left Portland."

"Did you date down here?"

"Hardly. To begin with, she was homesick and welcomed the chance to hang with someone from Portland, but later she had no more time for me."

Andi studied him for a moment before she asked, "You said an acting career was her main reason for coming down. What else made her decide to move?"

"Since I don't know it for a fact and am basically guessing, I'd rather not say."

Andi remembered the advice Mrs. Huber had given her a long time ago. Her boss had said, "When you want information from a person unwilling to give it, instead of pressing further, say nothing and just stare. Sooner or later the person will break the silence and most likely will tell you what you want." So Andi did just that.

It worked! The basketball game had ended and the TV program switched to some reality show, but Andi's eyes stayed locked on Brent's.

He finally said, "I think she wanted to get away from her parents."

Andi was stunned. That was not the answer she had expected. So she said, "I was under the impression that Megan was close to her folks."

"Too close. They smothered her with love. I think that she needed to get out of their grip in order to breathe."

"Did she tell you that?"

"No. Like I said, it was just a gut feeling of mine."

The guys who had been interested in the Lakers game paid for their drinks and left. Soon their stools were taken over by a new set of clientele. Brent took their orders and was busy mixing drinks for a while.

As he faced Andi again she asked, "When was the last time you saw Megan?"

"I saw her on stage on the night she was killed."

"So you stayed in contact for the last two years?"

"We did not! Like I told you, we only hung out together when I first came to California. This February at the Cubbyhole Theater was the first time I saw her in over a year and a half."

"Was it by chance, or did you know that she was performing there?"

"Oh, I knew all right. I was real surprised when she called me up out of the blue inviting me to the play." And with a crooked grin he added, "She must have called every single person she'd ever met; the theater was packed full!"

"Did you talk to her after the performance?"

"Sure, I lined up with everyone else who wanted to get a peek at her up close and personal."

"Did you hear the explosion?"

"No, I missed it. Must've left the theater a short time before the bomb hit."

Andi could not think of anything else to ask so she finished her Ramos Fizz and inquired, "What do I owe you?"

"It's on the house."

Andi left the bar thinking, was that kindness or a bribe?

Chapter 25

Peter woke Regula up with a soft "Good morning" whisper into her ear, followed by a gentle back rub. Not fully conscious yet, she murmured, "This is nicer than the alarm clock."

It was R. A. Huber's turn in the driver seat, which suited her; she liked driving. Shortly after passing Redding, Interstate 5 was no longer a boring drag through endless flatland, but rather an ever changing tableau of hills, forests and mountains. The scenery became picturesque with the ascent to the Shasta Lakes, where a stretch of forest landscape gave way to a sudden view at majestic Mt. Shasta streaked with patches of snow. Getting closer, the stately peak presented itself from different angles. The sometimes curvy two-lane freeway - - trucks on the right and cars on the left - - wound around mountain terrain. The speed limit was 65 mph, except around curves. When, along the Klamath River, the limit was posted at 55 mph for no reason it seemed, and the woods got even denser, the pair realized that they must have crossed the California/Oregon border.

When they arrived in Eugene on Saturday late in the afternoon, they had driven 470 miles in seven and a half hours that day and were well into the state of Oregon. They found accommodations for the night and then headed to downtown Eugene on foot to explore the area. There was a pleasant river walk for the first leg. The temperature was in the low 60's and getting colder by the minute, so they were glad to have jackets. The University of Oregon was located smack in the center of town. Kids hung out everywhere and many rode their bicycles on the sidewalks, but the Hubers seemed the only pedestrians out for a brisk walk.

In the evening, Huber called Andi, who clued her in on the interview with Brent Halifax.

Huber heard her out and then said, "So he was cooperative?"

"Sure thing, boss. A little hostile at first, but he soon loosened up."

"Do you believe his statement about not following Megan to California?"

"I'm not sure what I believe."

"His take on the parents is interesting. I'll keep it in mind when I talk to them on Monday. Oh, and Andi, did you get a hold of Ralph Weatherford?"

"Not yet, ma'am."

"Keep trying."

Next morning, they tanked up before starting on the last 120 miles toward their destination. To their great surprise, Oregon still provided full service at gas stations. The attendant filled the tank and washed the widows, while they sat inside the car and watched him work.

Peter said, "Do you remember when they did this in Southern California?"

"Barely, it was so long ago," his spouse replied.

When snow-covered Mt. Hood appeared on the horizon, it was clear they were fast approaching Portland. The time was only 11:00 a.m. as they drove into the parking lot of a Best Western located along I-5, so they had all of Sunday to themselves to explore the fascinating city.

After booking a room for two nights and a bit of freshening up, they walked to the nearest train station and boarded the Yellow Line for downtown. They got off at 1st Street and Oak, and then strolled the length of the waterfront along the lovely river walk, admiring the many bridges crossing over the Willamette River, each one different in design. Next they ambled over to Chinatown. It was rather small, about three blocks square. Sadly, the historic buildings were in decay. They walked on. About ten blocks farther, they happened upon the Pearl District. That part of town captivated their fancy with its variety of antique stores, art galleries and cafes. The old buildings looked marvelously preserved. Peter snapped a few pictures of a particularly interesting structure that came to a point where two streets met, reminding them of the Times Square building in New York City.

By chance they came upon Powell's book store, where Peter entered book heaven! The place was overwhelming. It was three stories high and each floor had several large rooms filled to the brim with books. The rooms were named by colors; i.e., Blue Room, Red Room, Orange Room, Pink Room, and so forth, and the bookshelf aisles were numbered. The store sold both new and used books, some of the old volumes costing much more than when new. In each of the rooms sat an employee behind an information desk, directing people to a certain area or aisle if they needed assistance. And if one asked for a book out of the ordinary, he or she would look it up on their computer. Peter even spotted two of his own works in the Orange Room. They spent one and a half hours in the place and left with four books, a new address book, and postcards.

Towards evening, they trekked back down to the river. There were many restaurants to choose from at the marina. They dined at McCormick and Schmick's, where they savored a delicious meal of tilapia for him and swordfish for her. The return walk to the train station along the waterfront was a treat after dark. They marveled at the reflections of lights on the water coming from restaurants, bridges and boats anchored in the harbor.

Before turning out the lights on that Sunday night Peter said, "So Regula, tomorrow you'll start working, right?"

"No doubt. And what are your plans?"

"Oh, I'll find a way to pass the time."

She smiled and remarked, "One and a half hours wasn't enough for you, huh?"

"I can't keep anything a secret!"

Chapter 26

On impulse, Andi decided to see *From Sin to Virtue* on Sunday night. She arrived at the Cubbyhole in plenty of time to purchase a center orchestra seat ticket and read the program before curtain. As show time drew near, it became evident that the play had lost some of its popularity; there were a few empty seats scattered throughout the theater. Andi spotted a couple of security guys in the audience. They were plain clothed, but the way they scanned the crowd with trained eyes, along with their physiques, gave them away. Good to know, Andi noted to herself. In another minute the lights dimmed, people hushed, and the curtain went up.

The essence of the play was a battle of good versus evil. The characters were represented as the seven capital vices against the seven virtues. The main plot amounted to a tug of war between these forces with clever side plots thrown in to keep the show lively as well as intriguing.

Andi sat close enough to the stage to see the expressions on the actors' faces. She watched Todd Brighton as character Pride, dressed in a devil's costume, applying endless charm to lure his victims into following the path to wickedness. He suddenly spotted the redhead in the audience and promptly winked at her. Mercedes Cleveland gave a stunning performance as Mother Earth, and Adriana Rippling, in the role of Vanity, threw Andi an angry glance. Holy Krewe, Andi thought, does she still think I'm after her part? Chad Lindhurst was steadfast in his portrayal of Fortitude and never made eye contact with her.

At intermission she overheard the conversation between two women seated immediately behind her. The first said, "They might be amateurs, but I'm impressed with their acting." The other remarked, "I heard that the original Vanity was better; she blew everyone away. Oops! I shouldn't have said that since she ended up getting blown away herself."

When the play continued, its pace picked up, keeping the audience spellbound until the climax of the dramatic ending as Vanity was brought to her knees. In general, Andi was not keen on drama plays; she preferred musicals. Still, as she walked out of the auditorium she was bowled over by *From Sin to Virtue*. In the lobby the cast members mingled with spectators. Most folks crowded around the lead characters, including Vanity, Pride, Greed, Lust, Justice, Fortitude, and Mother Earth.

Andi, forever rooting for the underdog, went over to the less prominent characters Envy and Anger and said, "Ya'll did a great job! You made me feel the emotions."

Flattered, they replied, "Thank you so much!"

Over their heads, the character Vanity, who was busy talking to a fan a few yards away, gave her the evil eye. Andi took it with a grain of salt and headed for the crowded ladies room.

Ten minutes later, she walked to the parking lot. From a distance she noticed that a guy was ogling her Harley. Getting close, she realized that it was Todd Brighton.

He was grinning from ear to ear and said, "I had a feeling this was yours. I don't know much about Harley-Davidsons, but it looks special."

"You betcha! It's a 1990 FXR Super Glide."

With a mocking smirk he said, "How does a skinny girl like you handle such a powerful machine?"

"One mile at a time."

"I like your wit!" Then he asked, "Did you enjoy the play?"

"Yes, sir, I sure did." And with an appreciative nod she added, "That rope stunt getting you to hell and back was impressive!"

"My high school talents as a gymnast come in handy at times."

Then he became serious. "Tell me the truth; did you come to see the play or to snoop?"

"I reckon a little of both."

With an enticing smile he asked, "Do you have time for a cup of coffee somewhere?"

Before she could answer, Chad Lindhurst walked by on the way to his car and cut in, "Ms. LeJeune, is this man bothering you?"

"Thanks for the concern, sir, but he suggested nothin' I couldn't handle."

And without another word, she donned her helmet, swung one long leg over the saddle, kicked the kickstand up, hit the starter button and put her bike into gear. Then she waved to them as she rode off. The two actors stared after her, neither having scored a point in his favor.

Chapter 27

Eileen Maguire had proposed a midday appointment so that her husband would be on his lunch break and home for the interview. She had given easy-to-follow directions to their residence in South Portland, and Huber had no trouble finding the cottage style house.

When talking with the Maguires on the phone, Huber had had a vague impression of a couple in their forties demanding justice for their daughter's brutal end. Detecting an Irish brogue in their speech, she had imagined Owen in a tweed cap and Eileen dressed in green against a background of shamrock wallpaper. The folks who welcomed her into their modest home were closer to her own age and seemed frail and helpless. Both were clad in black; whether by coincidence or to make a mourning statement was hard to determine.

They ushered Huber into the living room, where she chose an armchair to sit on and accepted an offer of tea. While the lady of the house went to the kitchen to pour it, Owen sat down on the sofa facing her but made no attempt at conversation.

Huber said, "Please, Mr. Maguire, feel free to have your lunch; I know your time is limited before you'll have to return to work."

"I already ate." He was about to get up again and said, "Let me get my checkbook. What do we owe you so far?"

"Oh, don't bother. I will send you a detailed invoice in the mail." Then she inquired, "You work in a beer brewery, correct?"

He nodded. "It's just a few blocks down the street."

Eileen brought a tray with three cups of tea, sugar and milk, arranging it all on the coffee table. Then she sat down next to her husband and commented, "Owen is retiring in the fall."

There was deep sorrow in his voice when he said, "I was looking forward to it and dreamed of traveling once work was behind me, but now I've lost the desire."

His spouse reached over and touched his arm, saying, "Megan was our pride and joy. Nothing seems to matter now that she's gone."

"I'm so sorry for your loss."

Eileen pulled herself together and said, "We're not fishing for sympathy. Thank you for taking on the case, and we appreciate that you drove up to see us. John said that you are an excellent investigator."

Huber was puzzled for a second and thought, who is John? Then she caught on and remarked, "Sergeant Wolf has helped me with many cases over the years, and I'm glad for the opportunity to return the favor."

Owen looked Huber straight in the eye and asked, "Are you making any progress?"

"My assistant and I have interviewed many people who shared Megan's California life, and we're planning to talk to some more. One and all are treated as potential suspects until proven otherwise. We have gathered lots of information, but it takes time to sort it all out. Learning more about the kind of person your daughter was would help a great deal, and I feel that you two can give me the most accurate account."

"Ask anything you like."

"I know that Megan was born and raised in Portland, that she dropped out of college and moved to Southern California, and that she was 22 years old when she died. I'd like you to tell me what she was like as a child, why she quit college, and what prompted her to move."

Eileen answered, "She was a lovable child, outgoing and smart. We had her late in life; our baby was sort of a miracle. Being the one and only offspring made her the center of our lives, and I'll admit that we spoiled her. Elementary and high school was a breeze for our Megan; she got good grades and was popular. When she joined the drama club in high school, we enjoyed watching the plays she performed in, but had no idea she was seriously considering an acting career."

A tear rolled down Eileen's face, and Owen took over, saying, "We watched our pennies to save up so we could send her to college. She enrolled right here at the University of Portland, a private Roman Catholic university, aiming at a liberal arts degree. She seemed happy as a freshman, but halfway into her sophomore year she talked of quitting."

"Do you know why?"

His wife said, "Megan didn't say, but a mother knows. It was because of that unfortunate young man who followed her around. She dated him for a while, but when she broke it off, he would not take no for an answer. He pestered her until she felt that leaving town was the only way to get rid of him."

Huber asked, "Would that be Brent Halifax?"

"So you've heard of him. He even followed her to California."

"My assistant, Andi, talked to Brent the other night and he tells a different story."

Owen said, "Eileen, be honest. The real reason Megan dropped out of college and moved to California was in pursuit of an acting career."

Eileen gave her tears free run now and cried out, "I knew nothing good would come from her joining the theater world. And look what happened!"

"You feared for her life?"

"Of course not, or I would've found a way to stop her. I meant that I was concerned for her morals. Mixing with that crowd is a bad influence, I'm sure."

"You came to see Megan perform on opening night of the play, *From Sin to Virtue,* correct?"

"That's right. She invited us down, and even though we had reservations about her becoming an actress, it's only natural that we supported her and came to see her perform. We made a vacation out of it and had a lovely drive down the coast. The play was enjoyable and Megan was great as Vanity." She glanced at her husband and said, "Wasn't she, Owen?"

He said, "Yes, dear."

Eileen sighed and continued, "Afterwards, Megan told us to wait for her in the theater lobby while she changed into street clothes. We were going to take her out for a nightcap to celebrate. And then the horrible thing happened. When we heard the bang and felt the floor shake under our feet, we didn't know what was going on. There was still a small crowd gathered in the lobby and everyone seemed disoriented at first. A few people went back into the auditorium, but most ran out of the theater in a panic. Owen and I decided to stay put in the lobby; after all, that was where Megan would come looking for us, we thought."

She took a deep breath and continued, "Then someone walked by us and exclaimed that an explosion had taken place backstage and had blown a performer's dressing room to pieces. 'Which performer?' I asked with a heavy heart. The person replied, 'The one who plays Vanity.' I cried out, 'Lord Almighty, that's our Megan!'"

She shuddered. "It's still all a nightmare. We tried to get backstage, but the police had already cordoned the entire area off with crime tape and wouldn't let us through." She wiped her eyes and said, "Well, you know the rest."

Owen checked the time and got to his feet. He extended his hand to Huber and said, "I need to get going."

She shook it, saying, "I know the interview was difficult for you. Take care."

Then he bent over his wife, pecked her on the cheek, and was gone.

When the door closed behind him, Eileen remarked, "He never wants to talk about it and keeps it all inside. He'll burst wide open one of these days."

Huber glanced over to the mantel where there was a family picture displayed. The snapshot was taken in happier days. A young woman, flanked by proud parents, was smiling into the camera.

Huber said, "This was Megan?"

Eileen nodded and took the framed photo down from the mantel and handed it over. The lady detective was told on several occasions that Megan had been lovely to look at, and the picture proved it. What startled her, though, were the images of the parents.

She asked, "When was this taken?"

"Last November when Megan flew home for Thanksgiving."

It was shocking to see the change in these people in just a few months. The couple had aged ten years and looked a shadow of their former selves. The picture showed healthy, happy parents delighting in their pride and joy. Now, Owen was stooped over like an old broken man, and his wife looked haggard, having lost several pounds she could not afford to lose.

Huber silently handed the picture back. Then she said, "You have a lovely home and I admired your garden before I rang the bell. Taking care of it must occupy a lot of your time. Am I correct in assuming you don't have a job outside the house?"

"That's right." And her face suddenly lit up when she added, "I do volunteer work at the International Rose Test Garden twice a week and love it. It's the only thing that keeps me sane these days."

"I've heard of the place. Is it nearby?"

"It's located inside Washington Park in Southwest Portland. The gardens are fabulous; you should take the time for a visit. There are over 7,000 rose plants of about 550 varieties. The roses start blooming now in April all the way through October. New rose cultivars are sent to the garden from all over the world for testing of color, fragrance, and disease resistance. Founded in 1917, ours is the oldest public rose test garden in the United States. In the beginning, as World War I was raging in Europe, hybridists sent roses from around the world to our garden for testing and to keep the new hybrids safe from being destroyed by the bombing in Europe."

She gave a quick stare to make sure she still had an interested listener and continued, "There are three main parts: the Royal Rosarian Garden, the Shakespeare Garden, and the Miniature Rose Garden. The first of these gardens honors the Royal Rosarian civic group, which serves as the official greeters and goodwill ambassadors for the City of Portland. The Shakespeare Garden is a favorite spot for weddings. Its focal point is a brick wall with a plaque of William Shakespeare's image and his quote, 'Of all flowers methinks a rose is best.' And the third is one of only six testing grounds for the American Rose Society miniature rose test program. The national annual winners are displayed in the center of this garden."

While describing the place where she volunteered, Eileen became animated, and it was clear to Huber that taking care of roses was her only distraction and therefore therapy in her grief.

She asked, "In which of these gardens do you work?"

"Wherever I'm needed. I'm not picky. Sometimes I even work as tour guide."

Steering the conversation back to the main subject, Huber said, "Talking with many people who shared Megan's life in California in one capacity or another, I got the impression that your daughter kept her feelings to herself. She did not seem to have been close to anyone."

"You're right about that. Our Megan was good at hiding her true feelings. That's probably why she was such a talented performer."

"How often did you hear from her?"

"She called us twice a week; usually Sundays and Wednesdays."

"Did she mention that she was worried or afraid in the days before she was killed?"

"She said no such thing."

"What did you make of her frame of mind the last time you saw her?"

"That would be the day of her premiere. She was excited about the play and pleased that we came down to see her for opening night."

"Did she ever comment on the people around her, like her roommate, her boss and coworkers, and the actors in her amateur theater group?"

Eileen briefly mulled it over and then replied, "When she first found an apartment she said that her roomie was a fitness freak and messy, but not to worry, she could handle her. About her employer she remarked that the woman was as French as they come, but interesting to work for. As for the theater group, she said that most had talent but that some of the young women were - -" she hesitated before she could bring herself to repeat the word "- - bitches."

"Can you remember anyone else she mentioned? I'm thinking of friends she might have made and men she dated."

"I don't think she made many friends; our Megan was reserved. Of course, I asked her about men; a mother wants to know. She went on dates with a few fellows, but nothing serious."

"Do you think she made enemies?"

"I can't imagine that she made enemies; everybody liked her. I've been thinking things over and over and can't come up with a reason for someone wanting to harm her. It must have been a dreadful mistake."

"Do you know if Megan kept in contact with friends here in Portland?"

"For sure she kept in touch with her best friend, Hailey. The two were always inseparable. Actually, Hailey has been a big comfort to me lately. She calls often to find out how Owen and I are doing, and stops by for a visit now and then."

"What is Hailey's last name, and do you happen to have her phone number?"

"The name is Tuckfield. She used to live on the next street, but moved to a different part of Portland after getting married." And without any hesitation, she handed over Hailey's phone number and address.

Huber thanked her, got up to leave and stated, "I will do my very best to find Megan's killer."

Chapter 28

Seated at a window table overlooking the Willamette River in an Italian restaurant, Regula told Peter all about the interview with the Maguires over a delicious Spaghetti Napolitano dinner.

Peter said, "They sound like total wrecks."

"Yes, they're both suffering, but Owen is hit the hardest."

"Why do you think that?"

"Eileen can cry, plus she has her International Rose Test Garden to distract her."

"I see what you mean. The man is working at a beer brewery, you said?"

"Correct. And why are you grinning?"

"Something strikes me funny, that's all."

"Out with it!"

"I find it amusing that both are connected to nicknames of the town."

"You're making no sense, Peter."

"Let me explain. At Powell's bookstore today I leafed through a coffee table book about Portland. The town has two official nicknames: number one, *City of Roses*, and number two, *Beertown*, as there are numerous beer breweries in the area."

Then he got serious and asked, "So did you learn more about who Megan was?"

"In a way, but I'm more confused than ever what really made her tick."

"Come again?"

"Okay, here is a young woman who seemed to need her space. I don't think her parents knew what was going on in her head. To them, she was still the little girl they raised, and they either couldn't or wouldn't look beyond. So far that is all clear to me; happens all the time in the best of families. Then she moved to California and got her freedom. And here is what I find paradox: The young woman called her parents twice a week and hardly made any friends in her new world over the span of two years."

"I see what you mean now."

The waitress cleared their plates and asked, "Do you care for dessert?"

They replied in unison, "No thanks, just coffee, please."

Moments later, Regula sipped her brew while glancing out the window. The restaurant's lights mirrored in the water and the anchored boats in the harbor swaying in the breeze should have had a soothing effect on her, but she could not relax.

Peter said, "You're frustrated as heck!"

"Is it that obvious? You're right. This case is a brainteaser. I thought that by now I'd have a clear profile of Megan which should help me find a motive for her murder, but I haven't made much progress."

"You'll get there; you always do."

"Thanks for the confidence!"

Then he asked, "So what are we doing tomorrow?"

"I have an appointment to see Hailey Tuckfield in the morning. At this point, I'm putting all my eggs in her basket. And after that, we can drive home."

"Sounds like a good plan to me. And now, let's go for a stroll on the riverbank and forget about Megan Maguire."

For the next twenty minutes his spouse was able to enjoy the moment, but when they got close to the train station her cell phone rang:

"Hi there, Mrs. Huber, hope I'm not intrudin' on ya'all."

"Not a bit, Andi. What's up?"

"That theater critic guy, Ralph Weatherford, refuses to give me an interview."

"What?"

"I reckon he got pissed off by my many messages. He called this evening madder than a hornet, telling me to go pound sand. In my last voice mail message I mentioned that I'd be willing to meet him at his office, his home, or anywhere else he'd prefer. He took this the wrong way and told me, 'I have nothing to say to you; not at home, the office nor in hell. So bug off.'"

Huber heard her take a deep breath before she added, "Sorry, boss, I've let you down."

"You did nothing wrong, Andi. Don't blame yourself and don't worry. We'll figure out a way to get to him once I'm back in town."

After they ended the call Peter asked, "Anything wrong?"

"Nothing major; just another road block. What else is new?"

Chapter 29

On Tuesday morning, R. A. Huber stood at Hailey Tuckfield's front door and pressed the doorbell for the second time. No one answered and she did not detect any movement from within the house. She glanced at her wristwatch; it was 9:30 a.m. Hailey had asked her to come by between nine and ten.

She turned away, ready to check out the backyard, when she heard a pleasant voice call out, "I'm in the shop!"

The sound seemed to have come from a separate small structure, and Huber followed the short pathway in that direction. The door to it stood wide open and she peeked inside. Along each wall were shelves holding craft materials and finished products. In the center of the room stood a long workbench, at the end of which a young woman, obviously greatly pregnant, was bent over a project. She appeared the all-American, girl-next-door type with light eyes, dirty-blond hair, a freckled button nose, and a cheerful, bubbly disposition.

Without looking up from her task, she said, "Come on in. I hope you don't mind if I keep at this for a few more minutes. I just poured water over the instant papier-mâché powder and need to mix and work with it before it dries up on me."

Huber entered. "Hailey?"

"Yep, that's me."

"I'm R. A. Huber and it looks like I've arrived at Santa's Workshop!"

Hailey laughed and replied, "I sure have the belly to prove it."

"So this is your studio?"

"Not really. It used to be a detached garage, and my husband converted it into a shop for me."

"Well, it's impressive. May I look around? I promise I won't touch anything."

"Be my guest."

There were shelves holding wooden dowels of different sizes; wire, acrylic paint, felt and fabric of all colors; lace and ribbons; see-through boxes filled with beads, glitter, and Styrofoam balls and eggs. Huber bypassed the racks of craft materials and browsed through the finished handmade items arranged on the shelves. A variety of ornaments sat in a display case. Some had Christmas scenes painted on clear glass; others were made of Styrofoam wrapped in gold thread and decorated with beads and tiny jewels.

She admired Santa Clauses of all sizes with exquisitely crafted faces. An old-fashioned Santa candy holder made with toilet paper rolls caught her eye. There was an array of sleighs filled with miniature toys. Intricately detailed Christmas trees, approximately 12 inches in height, were standing under glass domes. Beads and pearls hanging from thin wire hooks served as the trees' ornaments, and fancy custom jewels adorned their tops, while tiny toys formed a circle around the foot of each.

Huber walked back to the workbench and watched the young woman at her handiwork. Now wet, the papier-mâché had the consistency of oatmeal. She shaped the dough into a ball by patting it with her hands.

"What are you making?"

"Santa's head that'll go on his body over there," and Hailey motioned with her chin in the direction of a headless figure on the workbench a few feet away.

Then she worked with total concentration on the ball in her hands. When satisfied with the shape of the head, she formed the face with her fingernails and a toothpick. It was intriguing to watch as cheeks, nose, eyes, lips, and ears came into being. Finally, she poked a dowel into the bottom of the head and stuck it into a piece of Styrofoam.

She said, "Okay, I can leave the head alone now. In a couple of days it will be dry enough to paint."

"What kind of paint do you work with?"

"I use acrylic paint, and then apply clear fingernail polish on the eyeballs to make them glisten." And she showed Huber a piece of mohair for the beard, already cut and shaped.

Then she explained, "After the face is painted and has dried, I'll attach the head by placing it on the armature wire sticking out of the body. Then I'll glue on his hair and beard. The last thing I'll do is attach Santa's collar and put on his hood."

Huber looked over to where the body part lay dressed in a red suit and remarked, "That's a good-size Santa you're making!"

"He'll stand at 25 inches tall when finished. I've made larger ones, though."

"So how do you construct the body?"

"I start with an armature. Some armatures I make with wooden dowels and others, like the one for this Santa, I form with heavy gage wire. Sometimes I purchase ready-made plastic armatures which come with flexible arms and legs. Anyhow, I twist the wire to form body, arms and legs. Then I cut felt pieces into shape for the body and limbs, stuff it with cotton batting, and stitch it closed. You can see part of the armature wire sticking out on top of the body. That's to attach the head later."

Huber pointed to the collection of Santa Clauses on the shelf and asked, "Their heads and faces are all made from papier-mâché?"

"Not all of them. On some I've used Sculpy-Clay, which is polymer clay that's baked in the oven. And a few I've made from a Styrofoam egg by carving it into a head shape, sticking cotton on it, and then taking a nylon stocking and pushing creases to shape the face."

"Sounds like a complicated process."

"It's a bit tricky, but doable."

"I've noticed that some beards look different. What do you use besides mohair to make them?"

"They're also made from fake fur, rabbit fur or hair left over from old doll wigs."

Huber pointed out an assortment of smaller Santa figures and inquired, "How did you make these?"

Hailey replied, "Those are Plaster of Paris faces. They're real easy to do. You use candy molds or any flexible plastic molds to make the faces and then just pop them out. Then all you have to do is paint them."

Huber nodded her head appreciatively and said, "You've got a great business going here!"

Hailey giggled and replied, "It started out as a hobby, but then I decided that I might as well make a little profit out of my crafts."

"How do you go about selling your treasures?"

"Mostly on the Web; thank God for E-Bay! And during the Christmas season a local store carries some of my items on consignment"

All of a sudden Hailey rubbed her belly and stated, "I need to sit down; let's get out of here."

Chapter 30

They entered the house through the back door and then Huber followed Hailey into the living room. The young woman supported her back with both hands as she walked and then plopped into an upholstered chair, motioning Huber into another.

Huber asked, "Your back hurts?"

"Yeah, that comes with the territory, I'm told."

"When are you due?"

"Any day now. The nursery is ready, and - -" she tapped her belly "- - I'm more than ready!"

"What are you having?"

"A boy, and we'll name him Alexander."

"Now tell me about Megan."

Hailey smiled and said, "After all, that's why you came to see me!" Then she became somber and shared, "I miss her. She was my best friend."

"How long was the friendship?"

"Forever!"

"Which means?"

"Since kindergarten."

"I bet you knew her better than even her parents did."

"They didn't know her at all. At least not since she grew up."

Huber commented, "That was my feeling also. So what was she like?"

"Megan was clever, in total control of her emotions, ambitious, loyal, secretive, a perfectionist, curious, and had plenty of self-esteem. People who didn't know her thought she was stuck-up."

"But that wasn't so?"

"Nope. She was sure of herself, but that's not the same as conceited."

"Was she popular in high school?"

"Sure. Everyone wanted to be friends with her, so she hung with many different groups of kids. She could take 'em or leave 'em, though, and never got real close to anybody."

"Except you?"

"Yeah, Megan and I were tight."

"Did she have many boyfriends?"

"Boys were in awe of her, and she could've had just about any boyfriend she'd wanted, but Megan was picky. She didn't miss a single school dance and got herself a new date for each occasion, but never had a steady boyfriend throughout high school."

"What about college? Did you go to the same school?"

"No, she went to the University of Portland, and I did my two years at the Community College, ending up with an associate degree in Graphic Design."

"You kept in touch, though?"

"Definitely. We saw each other at least once during the week and spent many weekends together."

"Did she date different young men while in college?"

"At the beginning, yes, and then we did mostly double dating; she and her boyfriend, me and Kyle." She added, "That's my husband, but we weren't married then."

"Was her boyfriend Brent Halifax?"

She gave a cheerful giggle and answered, "You've done your homework!"

"Do you know why they broke up?"

"Brent wanted more from Megan than she was willing to give."

"A commitment?"

"Yeah, among other things."

"Did she tell you her reason for quitting school and moving to California?"

Hailey gave her a bittersweet smile and remarked, "She didn't have to; I knew what went on in her head. It was a combination of things. She wanted an acting career more than anything in this world. Her parents loved her so much, they didn't give her any space. They also tried to discourage her from entering the entertainment world, which made her even more determined. Then Brent, the idiot, smothered her with his devotion as well. She felt trapped from all sides."

Huber said, "I'm beginning to understand." Then she asked, "When you stated Megan's characteristics just now, what did you mean by her being 'secretive' and 'curious'?"

"Ah, you've hit on one of her complex traits. She was not open about herself and her own life, but enjoyed ferreting out other people's secrets."

"How often did you see her after she left Portland?"

"She came home for the major holidays, like Thanksgiving, Christmas, Easter, and my wedding. Megan was a gorgeous maid of honor."

"But you phoned one another on a regular basis, right?"

"Naturally."

"Mrs. Maguire told me that Megan phoned home twice a week. Do you think that she was homesick?"

"She called her parents more for their sake rather than out of her own need. And I think she missed Portland in a way, but I wouldn't call it homesick."

While Huber contemplated how to form the next question, Hailey tried to struggle out of her chair, saying, "I didn't even think of offering you anything to drink. What can I get for you?"

"Nothing, thank you. I had breakfast not long ago." So Hailey let herself fall back into her armchair.

Huber asked, "Did she talk to you about her new life and the people she was associated with in California?"

"Naturally she did. She had an impossible roommate, but Megan tried her best not to let it get to her. The fashion boutique she worked at sounded interesting and she enjoyed the job." With a little grin Hailey recalled, "She made me laugh hysterically when she mimicked her boss's French accent. And Megan admired her acting instructor to the point of worship."

"What about the people in her theater group?"

"As far as I know, she respected the director but was a tad afraid of him. She talked about a slew of actors, but these are the ones I could picture best. Todd she described as, 'he thinks he's God's gift to women.' She liked both Mercedes and Chad. She even dated Chad briefly. Megan wasn't bothered much by her understudy's jealousy. If anything, she was amused by it and thought it was hilarious how the woman hated her guts."

"Did she make any friends among these people?"

"She hung out with the group, but I don't think she got real close to any of them. I remember her telling me once, 'I don't trust anyone.'"

"What can you tell me about Brent Halifax?"

"He's harmless, in case you were thinking about him as the killer."

"I understand that you gave him Megan's number before he moved to California."

"That's true. I figured they might both enjoy having an old friend nearby. I knew that Megan would not consider dating him again, though."

Then Huber asked, "When was the last time you talked with Megan?"

"Let me think - - that was Wednesday before her play's premiere. I was all excited to fly down for it."

"So you saw her perform?"

She shook her head and stated, "I never made it."

"The airline didn't let you fly because you were pregnant?"

"No, that wasn't the problem. On my way to the airport on that Saturday, I went into false labor pains, so I asked my husband to drive to the hospital instead. I spent most of the day there, and by the time they let me out, it was too late to catch another plane to LAX and get to Pasadena in time for the play."

She sighed and continued, "In hindsight I feel guilty. Maybe if I'd seen her on Saturday and talked to her before the play, I could have insisted that she'd go to the police."

Surprised, Huber asked, "Did you get the feeling that she was afraid for her life when you had that last talk with her on Wednesday?"

"No, she didn't seem worried and didn't say anything about being in danger. It was on Friday, the day before the premiere, that she was texting me a weird message. It didn't make much sense. She wrote that she was wise to someone and debating whether to take the info to the police."

"What was her precise text message?"

"I can't remember the exact words. She mentioned something about a 'monkey' or 'monkeys' where they didn't belong, but I'm sure that was a typo. She must have meant 'money.' Anyhow, I texted her back, asking for clarification to which she answered with another texting, 'Never mind. I'll explain it all when you get here.'"

She shook her head and murmured, "If I'd been there, I might have prevented her from getting killed."

Huber was touched by the tremendous sadness in Hailey's eyes. She reached over and squeezed her hand, stating, "Even if you had taken Megan's allegations to the police that day, the outcome would have been the same. They would have promised to look into the matter, but I doubt that they could have stopped anyone from planting the bomb in Megan's dressing room that evening. I'm positive that the wheels had already been set in motion by that time. Short of being clairvoyant, there was nothing you could have done. No need to torture yourself with guilt."

"I guess you're right."

"Look to the future and think of all the joys baby Alexander will bring. You've got plenty of cause to be cheerful."

Hailey folded her hands over her large belly and smiled.

Chapter 31

In the afternoon, the Hubers were homeward bound. At the outskirts of Eugene they left Interstate 5, crossing over toward Florence on Highway 126. The Oregon coast was beautiful. They rode over many bridges, some of them spectacular in design. The drive led them along the ocean with sandy beaches and majestic boulders jutting out of the water, many the size of small mountains. At times the road veered inland through pine forests, then back along the water again.

After covering many miles in agreeable silence, Peter asked, "So how did the interview with the girlfriend go?"

His wife conveyed a short version of her morning at Hailey Tuckfield's residence, starting with "Santa's Workshop" and ending with the young woman's self reproach about having failed her friend by not being there on the crucial evening.

Peter listened carefully and then said, "Looks like you made some progress."

"In a way, yes. Hailey knew Megan better than any other person on this earth and gave me some insight into her mentality."

"At last you learned what made her tick; you must be pleased."

"I'm disappointed. I expected more."

"Come again?"

"Here is my point: The talk with Hailey confirmed a lot of things I already knew about Megan and explained some of the paradoxes. For instance, I learned that she called her parents twice a week out of loyalty rather than the urge to hear their voices. She was closest to Hailey, staying in steady contact with her, either by phone or text messaging. I can imagine that the two best friends told one another everything that went on in their lives. One of Megan's attributes was that she liked to uncover people's secrets. Since I'm unable to come up with another plausible motive for her murder, I'm assuming that the cause was for someone's self preservation. In other words, Megan saw or heard something that put her in danger. I was hoping that she'd let her friend know whom she was frightened of."

"She was going to do so on that Saturday."

"Exactly! If Hailey hadn't gone into false labor and had boarded that plane for California instead, I would not be investigating this murder."

"Regula, what are you saying? You don't believe that she could have stopped the killing."

"Certainly not, but Megan would have told her what she knew, and the case would have been easy for the police to solve."

Passing a bay, they spotted dozens of windsurfers. She remarked, "That looks like so much fun. If I were a few years younger, I might start windsurfing."

"That would not surprise me!"

Then she came back to the subject at hand and said, "I'm wondering about that last text message Hailey received from Megan. She thought that 'monkey' was a typo and should have read 'money,' but I'm not so sure. What if there is a connection with the monkey tail burglar?"

"That's food for thought."

"Precisely. Let me know if you come across another article in the paper about the burglaries."

Then she asked, "What did you do this morning?"

"I found a nice bench down by the river and got some writing done. And I called our Sunshine. She's expecting us tomorrow late afternoon, by the way."

"I'm anxious to see everybody; it's been four months already since Christmas. I can't wait to play with the grandkids!"

They stopped for the night at Brookings, the last town in Oregon before crossing the California border. The temperature in the early evening was 46 degrees with a tendency to drop even lower later at night. So they bundled up and went for a brisk walk and dinner.

Over a delicious enchilada meal Peter said, "I've been thinking. How important is an interview with the theater critic guy? I mean, he's not one of your suspects. Do you really expect that seeing him is going to help with your investigation?"

"Probably not, but I'm stubborn at this point. Ralph Weatherford treated Andi badly. I'll be darned if I'll let him get away with that."

Chapter 32

Another special meeting was held on Thursday night. When all were assembled in the hotel conference room, Member One called the meeting to order. Even before their leader opened his mouth, it was clear to everyone present that he was fuming.

He said, "For those of you who don't know, private investigators are looking into the Cubbyhole murder." And his voice was cold as ice as he continued, "What is the matter with you people? Why was I kept in the dark about this?"

As usual, he did not expect an answer and thundered on, "Had I known, I'd have canceled last week's job. I learned about the investigation by accident from a client."

Member Six protested, "Come now! We're talking about an old woman and a kid. What threat can they possibly be to us?"

Member One shot back, "You fool! I checked the woman out; she's good at what she does. She has a 98% success rate in solving her cases."

"That's hard to believe."

"Well, believe it! Never underestimate your adversary. Part of her strength is that she comes across as harmless and puts suspects off their guard."

Member Five spoke up. "I'm positive that we've given nothing away. The investigators haven't got a clue."

Member One countered, "I hope you're right for all our sakes." And glaring at the entire group he continued, "If any of you are questioned for the first time or as a follow up, be polite and cooperative, but don't volunteer information." And he looked directly at Members Five and Six as he went on, "And having contact with one another outside this room is strictly forbidden. Do I make myself clear?"

"Yes sir," was their unanimous response.

He turned to Member Seven and asked, "Are the art items from last Thursday's job still in your possession?"

"Yes, I didn't think it was safe to move them yet."

"Right, hold on to them until further notice."

He addressed Member Five and queried, "What about the jewels?"

"All under control," the latter replied.

Then Member One announced, "We have to cool it for a long time, maybe forever. All future jobs are herewith indefinitely suspended. There will be one last meeting in about two months to distribute the profit from the last heist. Look for the appropriate code sentence on the Yahoo group."

That said, he dismissed the members according to the usual protocol.

Chapter 33

For a few days Huber managed to push the Megan Maguire murder into the background of her mind. They had paid daughter Deborah and family, who lived in the Bay area, a visit on their way down the coast. It had been wonderful to spend some time with the grandchildren. Arriving at their house on Wednesday in the late afternoon, they had spent the night and then driven the long stretch home on Thursday. On Friday, she went to the gym, caught up with household chores, and Peter dropped his car off for major servicing.

When it was clear that he would not get his vehicle back until Monday, he asked his spouse to drive him to his signing event on Saturday, held at an independent bookstore located in the upscale shopping district in South Pasadena. Regula knew that he preferred for her not to be present at any of his author functions, be it a book signing, panel presentation, or a speaking/reading engagement. Somehow it was easier for him to talk about himself and his work in front of strangers without having his wife in the audience. She understood this perfectly but welcomed any opportunity to tease him about it.

She said, "No problem, I'm looking forward to it!"

"Oh, there won't be a need for you to stay; just drop me off."

"Aha Peter! You don't want me sticking around and making sure you behave yourself."

"You've got that right!"

She also touched base on Friday evening with Andi, who picked up on the second ring.

"Did ya'll have a nice trip home, Mrs. Huber?"

"The trip was fine, but I expected more from my interviews in Portland."

"You didn't pick much up from Megan's kinfolk nor from her friend?"

"I wouldn't say that. I learned a great deal, but am still in the dark as to how it can help with the investigation. You and I need to put our heads together sometime soon to sort it all out."

"Sure boss, whenever you say."

Then Huber remarked, "Sorry that you didn't get much of a spring break."

"I didn't mind, and I even did some partying the other night!"

"Good for you! How does your schedule look for Monday?"

"I have early classes and am free after two in the afternoon. Depending on traffic, I can make it to the office in an hour to an hour and a half."

"There's no need for you to ride to Pasadena. I'd like you to join me for the appointment with Ralph Weatherford at three o'clock at his office on the Westside."

"You're jivin'! You actually talked with the guy?"

"I did. When I put him on the spot about refusing you an interview, he claimed that it was all a misunderstanding."

"He came through loud and clear to me! Are you sure you want me to tag along?"

"Absolutely. We need to show a united front."

Chapter 34

On the way to Peter's book signing early Saturday afternoon, his wife asked, "Do you have time for a quick lunch?"

"No, I'm not hungry. And anyway, they usually have coffee and some snacks handy."

She parked the car and he leaned over to kiss her on the cheek, opened the passenger door and said, "If you're driving to the mall, come back for me in about two and a half hours."

She got out on her side and replied, "I'm not driving anywhere; I'll do some window shopping right here in this fancy neighborhood."

She strolled by a shoe store and eyeballed the latest fashions in high-heels. Huber had worn pumps of all kinds in her day, but these boasted eight-inch spiked heels. How anyone could walk on them without breaking at least one bone was beyond her. She lingered at the window display of a jewelry store, amusing herself with a little guessing game as to the values of the diamond rings exhibited. Needless to mention, no price tags were attached. Then she came upon a bistro and decided to have a bite to eat.

Huber was studying the menu when roaring laughter about jolted her out of her seat. I've heard that laugh before, she thought, and turned around. Two African American young women sat at the table immediately behind her. She did not know the lady facing her and was about to return her attention back to the menu, thinking that she had been mistaken. Then the other woman, whom Huber only had a back view of, turned her head, and there was instant recognition.

"Well, hello Mercedes!"

"Oh, it's Mrs. Huber. Welcome to my street!"

"Are you doing a little shopping?"

"I wish! Actually, I'm on my lunch break. I work next door at the jewelers. How is your investigation coming along?"

"It's progressing well."

"Good to know."

"Is *From Sin to Virtue* still playing?"

"You bet! And it won't be ending anytime soon. Well, got to get back to work. Enjoy your meal."

"And you break a leg tonight!"

As the two young women got up to leave, Huber thought, the investigation is progressing well? Whom am I kidding?

Lunch over with, she continued browsing the neighborhood. On the next block a young woman rushed out of a florist shop and collided with Huber.

"Oh, sorry! Are you all right?"

Huber rubbed her elbow and said, "Sure, no harm done." Then she did a double take and remarked, "I'm having a senior moment; where do I know you from?"

The young woman thought, senior moment my foot! You know damn well who I am.

Aloud she said, "I'm Adriana Rippling."

"Yes, of course! You've taken over Megan's part in the play." And with an engaging smile she inquired, "And what brings you to this neighborhood today?"

"I have to make a living, you know!"

Huber stared, seemingly at a loss.

"I've ordered flower arrangements for one of my jobs."

"Oh, I see. You're the wedding coordinator; how stupid of me not remembering. Well, you're obviously in a hurry so don't let me keep you. Have a good day!"

As the young woman darted off, Huber thought, Ms. Rippling was not pleased to see me, no doubt. Then she crossed the street and soon found herself standing in front of *Le Monde Fashion*. She admired a brand-new window display, equally eye-catching as the one she had been fascinated with less than two weeks ago. In this latest exhibit a clever pirate scene was depicted. Passersby could witness a sword battle in progress between crew and pirates on a sinking ship. And in the background was an island on which stood an open treasure chest with sparkling gems filled to the brim, some overflowing toward the ground. What gave the entire display a quirky and intriguing feeling was a long-legged modern young woman, dressed in the latest spring fashion. She was standing next to the treasure chest and gleefully eyed the jewels falling out of it.

Huber contemplated whether to enter the boutique. She thought, I probably can't afford to make a purchase but it's always fun to browse. On a whim, she opened the heavy door and stepped inside. The place was a lot busier than on her former visit. Angie was attending to customers and so was the other young salesclerk. For the moment, Huber was free to explore the merchandize on her own.

A strapless, silver metallic evening gown on a mannequin captivated her interest. The formal garment's attraction lay in the simplicity of its style and the elegance of the cut. She was touching the gown's hem to get a feel for the fabric when she overheard a conversation close by.

Someone said, "Have you heard what happened to the Rockwells?"

Another person replied, "About the burglary, you mean?"

"He made off with over $200,000 worth of booty."

"That's terrible, but I'm sure they carried insurance."

"Of course, but I understand that some of the jewels, like the Colombian emerald set, are irreplaceable."

"Oh, here comes Annette!"

Huber heard the distinct voice of Madame Dubois saying, "What are you two gossiping about?"

"Hi there, Annette. We were talking about the monkey tail burglar. You do know that he broke into the Rockwells' house?"

"Yes, I heard."

"You'd think that the police would have a clue by now. I guess the monkey is too smart for them."

Madame Dubois replied, "He is clever, that one!" Then she changed the subject and said, "Let me know if you wish to have Angie model something for you."

The two customers dispersed and Madame Dubois noticed Huber and walked toward her. There was a huge difference in the lady's appearance from their first meeting. Now her face was made up and her hair was pulled into a chignon. She wore a tailored dark grey suit and red pumps. Her skirt ended two inches above the knee, revealing shapely legs.

"Good afternoon, Madame Huber. Are you here on business, or may I show you our latest collection?"

"Just browsing. I was in the neighborhood and decided to stop by."

"Excellent. Let me know if you need help," and she moved on.

Chapter 35

"So how did the signing go?" Regula asked her husband on the drive home.

"I had a great time and sold a slew of books. I guess there is no evidence of a recession in this part of town. And how did you pass the time?"

"First I ran into a couple of suspects in the Megan Maguire case. One of them at least was not pleased to see me. And for the highlight of the day, I did a little shopping at *Le Monde Fashion*."

"You're putting us in the poorhouse!"

"Just about! I only bought a silk shawl, but spent a small fortune."

"Did you see the owner?"

"Yes, Madame Dubois was there. She looked every bit her part as the proprietress of a fashion boutique this time. There was also a gripping new pirate display in her window."

Peter remarked, "Pirate stories are popular at the moment. Your Madame Dubois is a good business woman."

"Oh, and the monkey tail burglar came up," and she related the conversation that she had overheard.

"That seems to be the talk of the town. I also heard it mentioned at the bookstore."

They drove without talking for a few miles and then she said, "My gut feeling tells me that there's a connection between the burglaries and Megan's murder, but I can't for the life of me see what it is."

Chapter 36

R. A. Huber and Andi met in front of Ralph Weatherford's office building. The directory in the lobby listed him as being on the fourth floor.

On the elevator ride up Andi asked, "Did you ever meet the guy?"

"No, but I heard that he's an eccentric, whatever that means. Most importantly though, he is held in high esteem in his profession as a theater critic and reviewer."

"His opinion is the stage Bible?"

"You could say that!"

They entered the reception area of his office, and before they made up their minds on which of the several Queen Anne wingback chairs to sit, a voice from within the inner sanctum sounded, "Come on in."

They approached through the open door, and beginning with the Persian rug thrown over a parquet floor, they had a virtual experience of being transported back to 17th and 18th century Europe. The room was a mélange of antique furniture and collectibles. There was a French Renaissance display cabinet with artifacts and knickknacks, such as a tall Normandy case clock, an 18th century French commode of solid walnut on which stood a sterling silver music box with an engraved Rococo design. A pair of antique armchairs with Aubusson tapestry stood next to a marble-top center table.

The walls were adorned with original antique French prints of frolicking Muses, an ornate gilded framed mirror, and an enormous hand-made tapestry wall-hanging. From the ceiling hung an Italian crystal beaded chandelier.

The only modern equipment was a computer, printer and phone placed on an antique oak Railroad desk, and a leather executive office chair.

Weatherford sat in that chair with his back turned to them, hammering away on his keyboard. He said, "Have a seat; be with you in a sec."

The only places to sit in the room were on the two tapestry chairs. The women looked at each other, and then Huber shrugged and seated herself in one. Andi made a "why not?" gesture and plopped down on the other.

Huber studied a vitrine on the marble top table next to them. It was constructed with a golden frame and glass sides all around, so that the pieces displayed could be admired from every angle. Within the vitrine she discovered an old-fashioned pocket watch, an ornate cigarette case, a couple of beautifully crafted rhinestone butterfly pins, and a few old coins.

She was about to put on her reading glasses to check the dates on the coins when Ralph Weatherford got up and walked over to them. He was a large man of about fifty, dressed in black trousers and a turquoise silk button down shirt. A heavy gold chain peeked out from his open collar. His face was round and clean-shaven and his brown hair was graying at the temples.

First he shook Huber's hand, saying the usual, "Pleased to meet you." And as he held Andi's hand in his, he announced, "I owe you an apology." He went to get his swivel chair and, rolling it over to where the women sat, continued, "You see, I thought you wanted to get to me for publicity reasons."

Andi said, "Sir, I don't follow."

"In your message you stated that you work for R. A. Huber Investigating. I logged on to the website and your name was not listed, so I didn't think you were legit."

"What did ya'll think I wanted from you?"

"I thought you might work for one of the tabloid magazines."

"No jivin'?"

"I wasn't alone on that evening at the Cubbyhole Theater. For myself, I could've cared less, but my date is not out of the closet."

"I gotcha now."

"As for me, I've been out for a long time." He chuckled and added, "Come to think of it, I was never *in* the closet."

Huber said, "You have a remarkable office!"

He replied, "I spend long hours in here; might as well enjoy what I'm looking at."

Then she felt it was time to get to the point and said, "Thank you for granting us an interview."

"I may not be able to help you, though. The young lady was unknown to me until I saw her perform as the character Vanity."

"I understand that Sal Silverberg suggested you should see *From Sin to Virtue.*"

"That's true. I usually pass on reviewing amateur plays, but when asked to do so by a director like Silverberg - - regardless of his retirement status - - I couldn't say no."

"Did you like the performances?"

"Some of the acting was good, but not all."

"And did you write a review?"

"I was going to, but under the circumstances I didn't have the heart to publish a not-so-favorable critique of Megan Maguire."

Astonished, Huber asked, "You didn't think Megan had talent?"

"Talent wasn't her problem; she had plenty of it."

Andi chimed in, "So what *was* the problem?"

"You've got to understand, I have high standards. I absolutely do not tolerate messing with lines."

Huber raised an eyebrow and stated, "Several people told me that Megan never forgot a line."

"She didn't forget a line; she changed it. I happen to know the last line of that play to the letter. The line is, 'I swear to God in heaven, justice is ultimately served!' And she butchered it to 'I swear to God and to the world, justice is ultimately served!'"

"I agree; she made a bizarre error with that line."

"Oh, I'm positive that it was *not* a mistake. She said it deliberately, enunciating each word."

"Why do you think she did that?"

"Beats me! Maybe she thought her version sounded better."

Then Huber asked, "Were you still there when the explosion hit?"

"No, I always make a point of leaving the theater at final curtain and never stick around to talk with the actors. They can read my opinion in the critic column." He added, "I went home that night and typed up my review, only to delete it next morning without having submitted it, when I learned of the news about the explosion."

Andi burst out, "That was kind-hearted of you!"

The sarcasm was not lost on him and he admitted, "After telling you to 'go pound sand,' I'm not surprised that you find it hard to believe that I can be kind."

There was nothing left to discuss, so the women thanked him for his time and took their leave.

On the elevator ride down Huber commented, "This thing about Megan changing her last line is puzzling. I need to have another talk with both Yuri Novokoff and Sal Silverberg."

And before they parted ways, she said, "Remind me to add you to my website!"

Chapter 37

On the next day Huber paid both the instructor and director a surprise visit. Neither was thrilled to see her. In the morning she stood in the hallway inside the Pasadena City College, waiting for the *Acting Fundamentals* class to come to an end. As young people hurried by on their way to and from classes, she kept a steady watch on the lecture hall door.

It suddenly flew open and a stream of students rushed out, nearly knocking her over. After the initial wave, they walked out in pairs or single file at a slower pace. As the last student came out, she peeked inside. With his back to her, Yuri Novokoff was busy gathering his video equipment.

She advanced into the room and walked toward him, making clip-clop noises with her pumps. He turned around and for an instant could not disguise his dismay at seeing her.

He recovered fast and said, "What brings you to my kingdom, Mrs. Huber?"

"Something came up and I'd like to discuss it with you. It will only take a few minutes. Can we go somewhere to talk?"

He shrugged, "Okay, I'll give you a few minutes. How about right here? The lecture hall is not being used for the next half hour."

"That's perfect."

"Have a seat; I'll join you in a minute."

Huber sat down in one of the front row chairs and watched him stowing his gear away. He was wearing another silk scarf, a blue one this time.   Must be his signature piece, she thought.

The instructor soon joined her and said, "So what's up?"

"I was wondering if you noticed that Megan changed her last line."

"I noticed nothing. What are you talking about?"

"Megan took out 'in heaven' from the text and replaced it with 'and to the world' in her last line of the play."

"I was unaware of it and am unfamiliar with the exact lines of *From Sin to Virtue*. I saw the play only once before on Broadway and that was a long time ago."

With a puzzled expression on his face he continued, "Why are you telling me this?   Did you see her performance?"

"No, but I talked with Ralph Weatherford yesterday."

"The reviewer?"

"Yes, he was at the Cubbyhole on that fatal night and - -"

"Wait a minute! Weatherford does not critique amateur plays, so why was he there?"

"The director asked him to come as a favor."

"I get it. Even the great Weatherford does not refuse Sal Silverberg."

"Anyhow, Mr. Weatherford noticed the discrepancy in Megan's last line."

Novokoff clicked his tongue in disgust and remarked, "He would, the nitpicker! Frankly, I have a hard time believing that Megan messed up. She always memorized her lines to perfection."

"He is of the opinion that Megan changed the words deliberately."

"Why would she do that?"

Huber stated, "That is the question I came to ask you."

"I have no idea," he replied.

Chapter 38

The hostess at *On Broadway* stuck her head in the door of Sal Silverberg's office and said, "The R. A. Huber woman is back to see you."

Annoyed, he looked up from his paperwork and asked, "What does she want?"

"She didn't say."

"Is she having lunch?"

"No, she just came to talk to you. I told her that you're busy so she said she'll wait."

He thought, what the hell does she want from me now? If I don't see her right away, she'll wait all day if need be. I might as well get it over with.

Aloud he said, "Show her in."

By the time the lady appeared, he had checked his ill temper and got up to great her. She took the chair offered to her in front of his desk, and he sat back down behind it.

He said, "I'm positive that I told you all I know concerning Megan the other day. And if you want to interview additional performers, you're on your own. I can't arrange another meeting with the cast."

"Oh, I wouldn't ask you to do that, and I'm sure you were open with me last time we spoke. Meanwhile, something came to my attention and I'm seeking your opinion."

"Shoot!"

"Apparently Megan changed her last line."

"How do *you* know?"

"I had an interview with Ralph Weatherford."

"The rascal! I wondered if he had noticed her tampering with the line."

"So you *were* aware of it?"

"Sure. The blunder was obvious. As a director one knows a play inside out."

"Mr. Weatherford was under the impression that Megan didn't misspeak, but that she changed the words on purpose."

"He's right. Megan knew her lines; she never once slipped at rehearsals."

Huber eyed him keenly and said, "So what was your reaction?"

Without hesitation he answered, "I was furious!"

"Furious?"

"You heard me. How dare she change a line to her liking? And she didn't even make it sound better: Why would anyone swear to *the world*? Ridiculous!" He went on, "I told you a little white lie the other day when I said that I was on my way backstage to congratulate everyone for a job well done when the bomb exploded. That was true for the rest of the cast, but I was going to chew Megan out for what she did to her last line."

"I don't blame you."

"I meant to demand that she tell me why she did it." He sighed and added, "Now I'll never know."

He stared into space without speaking for a long time. Huber did not mind the silence and looked around the room. Compared with the décor of the restaurant, his office was plain. Besides the desk and chairs there was a small bookshelf holding hardcover editions of gourmet and wine connoisseur books, a file cabinet, and a small refrigerator. On the walls hung French Country art prints. There was not a trace of the *On Broadway* flair of the restaurant just a few yards away.

He finally said, "Don't get me wrong; Megan was a fine performer and had the poise and looks to become a star.

Her goofing off was uncharacteristic and a disappointment to me."

Huber asked, "In retrospect, did you come up with a reason for her changing the line?"

He stated, "Following the explosion and after the authorities discovered Megan under the rubble, I completely forgot about it. At the time I had more important things on my mind. In fact, I didn't think about that last line business any longer until you brought it up just now."

"Well, if you figure it out, let me know."

Chapter 39

Toward the end of the day Huber and Andi huddled in a powwow at the former's office. They compared notes and Andi said, "At least we can cross Megan's parents who hired us, and her friend Hailey who wasn't in town, off the suspect list."

"I agree in Hailey's case. She was definitely in Portland at the time. As for the Maguires, considering them as possible suspects sounds absurd, but they were on the spot when the bomb went off and so we cannot dismiss them. I've been hired by the murderer himself before, remember?"

"Yes, ma'am. And I plumb forgot your rule: Everybody is a suspect until proven otherwise." Then she said, "If I recall everybody's statement correctly, most people were in the theater and could've activated the bomb with a few exceptions. Yuri Novokoff, Ralph Weatherford, and Brent Halifax left before it went off."

Huber remarked, "That's of no importance. It could have easily been detonated from outside the theater building. I presume a cell phone was used, and to people around the villain it must have appeared that he was making a call when he set it in motion."

"I reckon we best figure out possible motives." Scratching her red mane she declared, "I can't say that anyone had a plausible one, do you, boss?"

"I've been mulling over the motive angle for a long time without much success. Did I ever tell you about the main types of motives?"

"Can't say that you did."

"Aside from street crimes, gang-related shootings or stabbings, and serial killings, there are only three basic types of murder motives: One is greed, two is passion, and the third is for self-preservation."

"Interesting!"

"Tell me Andi, which of the three do you think applies to Megan's murder?"

"Well, I figure it's not likely greed or passion, so my pick is number three."

"That is also my opinion."

"So she knew something that was damaging to the killer?"

"That's the idea, and I have a theory. I take it that you've heard of the monkey tail burglar."

"Who hasn't?"

"Hailey told me that her friend mentioned something about monkeys in her last text message to her. I think that there's a connection between the monkey tail burglar and Megan's murder."

"Do I get this straight; you're taggin' the burglar as the killer?"

"Yes, and Peter thinks the burglaries are not carried out by a single person, but that there is a band of professional thieves at work. I tend to agree with him. There is such clockwork precision applied, that I've come to the conclusion the heists must be planned by a mastermind and executed by experts."

"So what about Megan?"

"I suspect that her killer is a burglar member. She may have seen or heard something that would have identified one or more members of the gang. Therefore she was silenced."

"Why didn't she take the info to the police?"

"According to that text to Hailey, she was thinking about doing so. I might be wrong, but my idea is that

Megan discovered whatever there was to discover close to the day of the premiere of her play. At the time she was preoccupied with her upcoming performance and put off going to the police. Yet I'm convinced that she knew she was in great danger. A chat I had with one of her neighbors and the episode he described made it clear to me early on in the investigation that she was frightened."

"You reckon she had a warning in mind by changing her line?"

Huber replied, "Either a warning or an accusation. I've been racking my brain trying to make sense of it. If it was meant as a finger-pointing, then she must have felt an immediate threat either by someone's words or action."

"So we need to figure out why she got rid of 'heaven' and added 'the world'."

"I've been trying to find the solution ever since Ralph Weatherford told us about the altered line and came up with a few scenarios, but none seem likely."

They kept quiet for a while, each following her own train of thought.

At last Andi said, "Sure thing, though; one of the folks we talked to has a profitable second income and is also Megan's murderer. How do we go about finding out who that is?"

Huber playfully made a move with the black knight on her chessboard. Then she put the figure back in its proper place and replied, "The situation calls for drastic measures."

Chapter 40

On the following day Huber was busy making arrangements. She called the Cubbyhole owners asking if she could borrow their theater for half an hour on Saturday morning. At first, Mr. Kingsley was reluctant to grant such an unusual request, but the lady detective used all her charm and persuasion, pointing out that a gathering of all people concerned was essential for her and Andi to solve the murder. When she argued that there could not be a better location for holding the meeting than the Cubbyhole where the tragedy had taken place, he gave in.

Next she sent a formal invitation to all parties involved. It read: "R. A. Huber and Antoinette LeJeune request the favor of your presence this coming Saturday at ten thirty in the morning at the Cubbyhole Theater in Pasadena for a presentation of the facts in the murder case of Megan Maguire."

Over dinner that evening she told Peter, "I'm going to stage a little performance of my own," and she explained her plans.

He asked, "What makes you think that all your suspects will show up?"

"There is no guarantee, but I'd expect that most will be curious enough to attend. In particular, the guilty person or persons cannot afford to stay away. He or they need to know what Andi and I have to say."

"So what do you expect from this performance of yours?"

'I'll poke around a bit and see what happens."

"Hoping that someone takes the bait?"

"You got it!"

"In other words, you'll be mostly bluffing?"

"You may call it that."

"And speculating?"

"That too."

"Be careful, Regula. Keep in mind how dangerous and unscrupulous your adversary is."

She grinned and said, "I'll be sure to carry my pistol at all times from Saturday onward, and if someone sends me flowers or an unexpected package, I'll be on the lookout for a potential lethal danger."

"It's not at all a joking matter," Peter replied.

Chapter 41

R. A. Huber and Andi greeted their "guests" in the Cubbyhole Theater lobby on Saturday morning, ushering them to the auditorium and asking each to take a seat in the first two center rows. As people trickled in one by one, a few showed apprehension, but most were curious about this unusual gathering. The invited actors made "don't know what this is all about" gestures at each other.

Amber Pierce thought, this better be good and not waste my time. I'd hate to have given up my aerobics this morning for nothing. And another thought crossed her mind; Megan would wallow in all this attention on her behalf were she still around.

Madame Dubois was decked out in one of her spring collections and wore an amused smirk on her face, in contrast to Brent Halifax, who turned up with a scowl on his. Silverberg and Novokoff entered together, a fact that made Huber wonder if they knew one another. A bewildered Mr. and Mrs. Kingsley stepped out of the theater office and joined the others in the auditorium. Except for Ralph Weatherford, everyone invited showed up for the occasion, but the lady detective had hardly counted on his attendance.

At precisely 10:30 the two sleuths stepped into the limelight.

Huber glanced out at the audience and exclaimed, "The stage sure looks different from up here!" Then she motioned to her assistant, "Come Andi, let's make this casual," and they both sat down at the edge of the stage leaving their legs dangling.

The senior sleuth started her spiel, "Thank you all for coming. We'd love to entertain with a bit of song and dance, right Andi?"

"Yes, ma' am. I'd be tickled pink to put on a show!"

Seated in the first row, Todd whispered to Mercedes next to him, "She's enjoying this; what a ham!"

Mercedes shot him an angry stare and hissed, "Shut up! I want to hear what the old woman is saying."

Huber had already continued with, "Unfortunately, we have a serious matter to put before you. I recently traveled to Portland Oregon to consult with Megan's parents. They are two broken people! We are asking for your help in solving Megan's murder so they will have closure."

She cleared her throat and continued, "I'm sure you've all heard of the monkey tail burglar. A friend of Megan's revealed a fact that makes us link our murder case to the burglaries. And I believe that the monkey tail burglar does not work alone but has a team of accomplices."

The lights were not dimmed in the front of the auditorium near the stage, so Huber had a clear view of her audience. She now watched their faces for a reaction. What she saw was mostly surprise, some indifference, and even a couple of amused expressions. She did not detect any look of dismay or panic. In other words, the guilty party kept a poker face.

She went on, "After getting back in town, another piece of important information came our way. I did not have the privilege to see Megan perform, but I am convinced that she gave us a vital clue on this very stage on her fatal night. I was made to understand by many of you that Megan was an excellent study and never missed a line. Knowing this, it stands to reason that the desperate young woman tried to make a statement and was actually asking for help by altering her last line. She said, 'I swear to God and to the world,' instead of 'I swear to God in heaven.'"

Huber paused, staring down her audience, and then said, "And here is where we need *your help*. Does the word 'world' ring a bell in connection with Megan? I imagine that it could have to do with the world at large, a globe, the universe, or the earth. Anything remotely relevant would assist us a great deal in solving the crime. Mull it over, and if you come up with something relating to 'the world' or any other information you think could be pertinent to our investigation, please contact us. I trust you've found my business card on your seats. You may stay anonymous if you wish."

She turned to Andi and asked, "Are there things I forgot to mention?"

The redhead proclaimed in her New Orleans drawl, "Just one: I want ya'll to know that gettin' in touch with us doesn't mean you're guilty. It'll only show that you've taken our plea to heart."

Then Huber made her last appeal "Think about it, please. If you have anything to contribute, you owe it to Megan and her parents to come forward. Thank you all for coming!"

Without another word the two investigators scrambled to their feet, moved to center stage, and took a bow.

As people filed out of the auditorium, Adriana said to her peers, "I wonder what they expect from this charade. I think the old lady is off her rocker."

Chad, who was walking toward the exit behind her, remarked, "You're wrong there; Mrs. Huber is quite sharp." And with a snide grin he added, "I'd watch my step if I were the killer."

Todd nudged Mercedes and teased, "So *Mother Earth*, any bright ideas what Megan tried to tell us with her word puzzle?"

"Oh shut up! You're not funny."

Amber rushed up the center aisle passing Madame Dubois and hissed, "Just like I thought; a total waste of time!"

"My sentiment exactly," the French lady agreed.

Yuri Novokoff and Sal Silverberg walked out together. The former asked, "What did you make of the investigators' performance?"

The director shrugged and said, "It was just that, a performance!"

Brent Halifax had a hard time controlling his anger as he stalked out of the theater and to his car. For this I drove all the way to Pasadena, he thought. Andi and her boss know nothing; it was all a farce.

The Kingsleys stayed in their seats a few moments longer after everyone else had left.

Mrs. Kingsley said, "The monkey tail burglar seems even more notorious than we realized!"

Chapter 42

Member Five arrived at Member Six's doorstep in a panic. The latter pulled the person inside and shut the door, yelling, "Are you crazy? I hope for both our sakes that nobody saw you!"

"I made sure that I wasn't followed. Besides, what difference does it make whether people see us together? Any future jobs have been canceled and Member One can't order us around any longer."

"You're not thinking straight! Never mind Member One, there are plenty of other reasons why we can't afford to be associated with each other at the moment."

Member Five shot back, "That's exactly why I'm here. Didn't you pay attention? That detective woman figured out that Megan was killed by members of the monkey tail burglars. She'll pin it on you and me at any moment now. We have to do something!"

"Calm down, will you? So she made the connection, which is unfortunate, but she has no specific facts, just some vague ideas. The lady has no clue as to who the members are, let alone who killed Megan. Why do you think she gave us that one-act performance this morning?"

Member Five shrugged.

"I'll tell you why. She was hoping to get a reaction from the people responsible and that they'd do something stupid. It's obvious that she succeeded; she has you panicked. We'll do absolutely nothing."

"She'll get wise to us, I'm positive. That's why I came to see you right away. We need to form a plan to get rid of her."

"Count me out! There's no chance in hell that we'd ever get away with wasting her. It's not only Huber, but also her wild-haired assistant we'd have to deal with. So forget it! Our best bet is to do nothing."

Member Five shot the other a venomous glance and insisted, "We can't just be sitting ducks. The woman asked for help, so I'll send her an anonymous note to divert her suspicions elsewhere until we come up with a better idea. Remember, we're in this together!"

"You're nuts. How anonymous do you suppose you can be? E-mail messages, phone calls, faxes, and even snail mail can be traced."

"Don't worry, I'll find a way."

"Member Six frowned and said, "Suit yourself, but put silencing the investigators out of your mind. I won't have anything to do with it. Do you hear?"

"Loud and clear!"

"And now, please leave and don't contact me at all for the next couple of months."

Chapter 43

There was a bit of response to Huber and Andi's performance. The director called and told Huber that, although he was not able to put Megan's last line out of his mind, he was so far unable to come up with a solution of what she could have tried to tell. He hoped that someone else who was at the Cubbyhole meeting would come forward with a useful idea. There was another phone call:

"Hi Mrs. Huber, it's Mercedes."

"Well hello! Have you thought of something that could help with the investigation?"

"No, but I'd like to point out, the fact that I'm the character *Mother Earth* means nothing as far as Megan's play on words goes. It's a coincidence and she certainly did not mean to accuse me."

"Thanks for making that clear. By the way, what *did* you think when you heard her change the line to 'the world' instead of 'in heaven'?"

"I didn't know she changed it until you mentioned the fact. Megan had the stage to herself; the rest of us waited in the green room. To tell you the truth, no one really listens to exact words in the last scene; we just anticipate the fall of the curtain and then rush to take our curtain call bows."

After they hung up Huber thought, so Megan was trying to make her statement to someone in the audience, or to the audience at large.

When she got to her office on Monday morning, she found a note pushed under the door, and it read, "I wouldn't know about this 'world' question of yours, but if

I were you, I'd take Adriana Rippling under scrutiny. She was fanatical about obtaining the part of Vanity."

The note was signed: "Anonymous."

Huber thought, I remember distinctly that many suspects told me, although jealous, Adriana would not have harmed Megan. Now one of them must have had a change of heart. That is indeed interesting!

The lady detective admitted to herself that she was disappointed. She had expected more of a reaction to their pitch. Granted, the anonymous letter was most likely written by the killer, but it didn't tell her a thing. She didn't bother attempting to find out where it came from as it was typed on a computer. The person who wrote it had tried to direct attention away from him or her by accusing Adriana. So Huber mused, this eliminates Adriana as the culprit. Unless she is extremely clever and wrote the note herself, thinking that I would jump to that conclusion. And the same applied for Mercedes. Drawing attention to the *Mother Earth* factor when she had to assume that Andi and I had already thought of it as a possibility was smart of her if she was the villain. And why did Sal Silverberg call at all when he clearly had nothing to contribute?

Maybe she needed to concentrate on the monkey tail burglars. Who of the suspects would be plausible members of a gang of thieves? She could not picture Mr. or Mrs. Kingsley breaking into residences of the rich and famous, cracking safes, identifying the most valuable jewelry and items, and taking off with the spoils in the dead of night. On the other hand, it might be possible that one or the other was the mastermind behind the burglaries. In that case the person need not be physically taking part in the break-ins. In Peter's opinion, the team of thieves consisted of experts in various fields. From that point of view, any and all of her suspects could be members of the gang.

She almost jumped when the phone rang. It was Peter.
He said, "Are you busy?"

"No, just frustrated. I can't get to the bottom of that
darn Megan Maguire murder. But never mind me. What's
up?"

"I just looked at my calendar. You're aware that we're
going to the fundraiser dinner tomorrow night?"

"Shucks, I forgot. And I've got nothing to wear!"

"Last time I checked, you had a closet full of frocks.
And as far as I know, it's just a dinner, not a fashion show."

"That's what *you* think."

As soon as they ended the call Huber yelled out loud,
Fashion show! I've got it! By George, I've got it!

Chapter 44

Minutes later Huber's excitement wore off and she thought, I know that I am finally on the right track, but how can we prove it? Our only hope is a gutsy surprise visit to the antagonist with a head-on confrontation. If we play it right, the person will feel cornered and talk.

She sent a text to Andi: "We have a break-through!"

As soon as Andi got out of class in the late afternoon she called and asked, "What's happenin' boss?"

"I finally caught on! How is your French?"

"Not as good as Daddy's used to be."

"Do you know what *'Le Monde'* means?"

"Yes, ma'am, it means 'the world.' Holy Krewe! You're talkin' *Le Monde Fashion*."

"Exactly! I can't understand what took me so long to see it."

"So that was Megan's point; she was accusing her employer."

"It certainly looks that way. I have it more or less figured out, but we'll need proof. You and I will pay Madame Dubois a visit and put her on the spot. Her window displays give out a revelation of their own. I reproach myself for not having grasped it before now."

"I don't follow you, Mrs. Huber."

"Never mind, I'll explain it all to you in person."

Andi said, "Think her boyfriend is in it too?"

"Absolutely. He might be our trump card when confronting her. I need to do some research on him and then you and I will put our heads together before we head over to South Pasadena. Make yourself available on a late afternoon or early evening someday soon."

"Want me to carry my piece, boss?"

"I don't think that'll be necessary. I'll have my .25 pistol handy just in case but hope that I won't be forced to use it."

"You think she'll talk?"

"I'm counting on it!"

Andi asked, "What's she like? I mean, you clued me in on what went down when you first interviewed her, but I'm curious to know who we're dealing with."

"I think petite Madame Dubois wears many hats. When I first went to see her, she was in the process of creating a new window display and seemed to be an interior decorator or an artist. When I dropped by her boutique recently, she looked and acted business chic, and last Saturday at the Cubbyhole, she was elegance personified." And with a chuckle she added, "Now that she is exposed as a member of the monkey tail burglars, I picture her in a slick skin-tight body suit on her nocturnal ventures."

"That's interesting but I meant, *what's she like*?"

"I see, you want to know what kind of person she is. I'd say that in that respect also she could be wearing more than one hat. Here is what I think of her: She can be charming, but I have the feeling she'd turn vicious when provoked. She's highly intelligent and shrewd, knowing exactly what she wants. The lady is a talented artist, has an excellent eye for fashion and is a superb business woman. I bet she takes risks, and it's likely that she's capable of killing."

"I have the feelin' she'll be a real handful when we tackle her."

"I imagine so. I'll get back to you as soon as I've developed the information on Chad Lindhurst."

Chapter 45

Madame Dubois was pacing amid racks of clothing and mannequins at her place of business. It was Tuesday evening, the doors of *Le Monde Fashion* had been closed to the public hours ago and her two employees had long gone home. The boutique's proprietress had been running on nervous energy ever since last Saturday, mulling things over in all her waking hours, which was most of the time, since sleep had not come easy.

Chad had been of no help whatsoever, and he made it clear that he would not lift a finger this time. The more she thought about his passive attitude, the angrier she got. After all, his neck was at stake too, even more so than her own. Writing that silly note had been a mistake, she now realized. She had reacted on impulse with that ridiculous attempt at distraction. And even though she was sure that it caused her no harm - - she had slipped the note under Huber's office door in the middle of the night with no witnesses - - it also accomplished nothing in her favor.

She paced from the store to the hallway, into the catwalk area, to her workshop, her office, and then back to the store again, while her mind was racing. She thought, that detective will catch on rather sooner than later, of that I'm certain. And when that time comes, she will show up here at my boutique to make sure she has all her facts straight. I'm a good judge of people, and I'd bet that is how the woman operates.

Madame Dubois mused further, never mind Chad. I need to protect myself and form a plan of action so that I'm prepared when the investigator shows up. Too bad that the burglaries had to come to an end. I knew from the beginning that the heists were not going to continue indefinitely, but had it not been for that nosy Megan, they would still be taking place. Oh well, it was fun while it lasted, she thought with a little smirk to herself. I was starting to get tired of bossy Member One anyhow.

Then she got dead serious again and went to her office to form a blueprint of how to get rid of the lady sleuth should the need arise. She worked out every detail, first in her head, and then she wrote it all down. With due attention to detail she re-read her instructions and revised them many times. When she was satisfied that there was no loophole left in her plan, she studied it with keen attention, memorizing every word. Then she fed the sheets of paper to the shredder. Lastly, she made a few minor preparations to get the place ready for her ploy.

It was past ten o'clock at night when she went home, thinking, I have it all planned out and it will work to perfection. I'll sleep well tonight!

Chapter 46

At the other end of town the Hubers drove home from the fundraiser.

Peter said, "You were awfully quiet this evening, Regula. Was it the food or the company?"

"Neither, I couldn't shake Madame Dubois from my mind."

"That's all! Want to unburden yourself?"

"It's just that I have so little to confront her with. Don't get me wrong, I'm positive that she and Chad Lindhurst are responsible for Megan's murder, but my evidence is all circumstantial. If she keeps her cool, Andy's and my bursting in on her may cause more harm than good to the investigation. I need her admission of the crime."

"But you're good at that!"

"What?"

"You're good at making people talk."

"She is clever, though, and unscrupulous. I have to be extremely careful of how I handle her. Our show could easily backfire. Now that we know who the villains are, I could never forgive myself if I botch up the investigation this late in the day."

Peter asked, "Who actually made the bomb and placed it in Megan's dressing room?"

"I'm sure that her boyfriend Chad constructed it; he's an explosives expert. And I also believe that he handed it over inside the orchid pot pretending to be the delivery guy from Champion Arrangements."

"So why don't you confront him, instead of the lady?"

"I think he acted on her instructions. If I read the woman right, she prefers giving orders rather than receiving them.

Besides, he is the cool and collected type; I doubt that we'd get him talking. But Madame Dubois is temperamental, I'm sure of that. We have a better chance of cornering her into incriminating herself."

"Be careful, Regula!"

"Don't worry; I'll have Andi with me, and my pistol."

Peter said, "I guess it would be useless of me trying to talk you into going to the police with the information you've got?"

"Absolutely useless! I have nothing to give them. My evidence is all circumstantial."

They had arrived at their residence in Merida, and driving the car into the garage, Peter said, "You're always at your best under pressure, so put it out of your mind for now and have a good night's sleep."

"Easy for you to say," his wife responded.

Chapter 47

The two sleuths stood in front of the window display at *Le Monde Fashion* pretending to admire the pirate scene and waited until the last two customers had left the boutique. Then they entered. It was five minutes before the store closed to the public.

The proprietress came to greet them, "Voilà Madame Huber. And this is Mademoiselle LeJeune, if I'm not mistaken. How may I be of service to you ladies?"

Huber said, "Hello there, Madame Dubois. I know it's late in the day, but my assistant and I came to - -"

Before she could finish her sentence Madame Dubois said loud enough for all in the store to hear, "No problem, I'll show you the collection myself!" Then she called to the young women who worked for her, "You may both go home. I will close the place."

After she had firmly locked the door behind her employees, she turned back to Huber and Andi with an apologetic smile and explained, "One has to keep appearances. It would not do for my help to know that I am under investigation."

"We understand."

She suddenly became extremely French and said, "You have more questions for me, yes?"

Huber replied, "A few, but we actually know a great deal already."

"Come then, let us go and be comfortable in the showroom," and she led the way out of the boutique, down the corridor along several doors, to the end of the hallway where she had them take a seat in the area where the modeling for clients took place.

"May I offer you a beverage? I have coffee, tea, or soda."

The investigators both declined and Madame Dubois pulled up a chair to face them. All stared into space for some moments.

Finally Madame Dubois blurted, "So you came to tell me something, *non*?"

Huber took charge and stated, "We've tied you to the monkey tail burglars, and what's more, we also know that you are responsible for the murder of Megan Maguire."

"That's outrageous! You have no proof for your allegations."

"On the contrary. Megan herself accused you by altering her last line in the play. She changed it to, 'I swear to God and to the world; justice is ultimately served!' By 'the world' she was pointing her finger at *Le Monde Fashion* and consequently at you, Madame Dubois."

"You call a dead woman's words proof? Ridiculous!"

"The dead girl's accusation was just a confirmation of what I had already been told by her best friend."

Perplexed, the French woman said, "And who is this friend? You already mentioned a friend of hers when you gave your speech on Saturday."

"Yes, it is that same friend who lives in Oregon. The name is not important, but the information we gathered from her is crucial. Megan was in contact with that friend on a daily basis. On Friday, the day before she was killed, Megan texted her suspicions of you to her confidante."

"What suspicions?"

"That you are the monkey tail burglar."

"The fantasies of a young woman are hardly evidence. You can't prove a thing."

"That's where you're wrong. I paid keen attention to your window displays; they tell the story and are evidence.

It is clear to us why you trust no one with your window dressing and tend to it all by yourself."

Madame Dubois started to lose ground and said nothing.

Andi spoke up. "Your boyfriend is already under investigation by the authorities."

"What do you mean?"

"They might give him a lesser sentence if he cooperates."

Madame Dubois turned to Huber and demanded, "What is she talking about?"

Huber took up her cue and stated, "It was easy to check his military record. Explosive specialists go through specific training."

"So what has that got to do with me?"

"You are a clever pair. You must have plotted your game plan together. And speaking of clever, it was extremely cunning of your Chad to mention in his interview with us that he'd dated Megan, just to show that he had nothing to hide. He knew we could have easily learned that piece of information on our own."

"He did what!"

"Oh sorry, I thought you knew."

Madame Dubois turned crimson with anger and the veins at her temples were throbbing dangerously. She said under her breath, "The louse!"

Outwardly she recovered fast and soon looked her composed self again, while the wheels in her mind turned at rapid speed. She thought, how dared he betray me with another woman, and with Megan of all people? The scumball! And for all I know he already has or will soon badmouth me to the police. Hell, two can play that game; I'll double-cross him.

She suddenly realized that no one had spoken for some time and that two pairs of eyes rested on her, scrutinizing every muscle in her face.

She said, "Okay, I'll tell it all, but let me make us some coffee first, it will only take a couple of minutes." She got up and asked, "Cream and sugar?"

Neither had a good excuse to refuse the offer and said "black" in unison.

"That's easy then, I'll take mine also *au naturel*." She was amused by her own choice of words, and giggled.

As soon as their hostess vanished down the hallway, Huber made a "don't drink it" gesture to Andi. The redhead had a "Holy Krewe" exclamation on her lips, but Huber put a silencing index finger to her mouth and the words never escaped Andi. She nodded her head in understanding instead. Soon Madame Dubois returned carrying a tray with three cups of coffee. She handed them out to her guests and took the last for herself.

Then she said, "All right, you seem to know a lot already. Where do you want me to start?"

If Huber had been in doubt so far whether their adversary had a lethal plan for them in mind, there was no question about it now. Why else would she cooperate without a struggle? She would bet that the danger lurked in the coffee. But then the woman might have plenty of other schemes up her sleeve. All this went through her head in seconds so that there was hardly a pause in the conversation.

She decided to take a shot in the dark and said, "Start at the beginning. About the monkeys that Megan was concerned about."

Madame Dubois replied, "Yes, that's what started it all. Megan was a snoop and the one time I forgot to lock the cupboard in my workshop, I caught her in the act of finding the monkeys."

"You mean the toy monkeys that were placed at the robbery scenes?"

"*Certainement*. I was in charge of them. Actually, leaving a monkey hanging by its tail after each accomplished job was originally my idea. Anyhow, I bought a number of toy monkeys and kept them in my workshop to have one handy for each heist. As I said, one day I walked in on Megan when she stood in front of the cupboard holding one of the monkeys in her hand. There was a guilty look on her face since she was obviously in forbidden territory. I told her off, informing her that she had better stop her snooping or find herself another job. She apologized and promised that it would never happen again. At the time I thought that was the end of it.

"Soon afterwards there was an article in the paper about the monkey tail burglar and she must have read it. It showed a close-up picture of the monkey left behind at the scene of the crime. She was smart, that one, and made the connection. From then on, she looked at me sideways. On Friday, the day before her premiere, I came back to my store after a lunch break and found Megan outside, staring at the display in the window. When she averted her eyes and looked straight into mine, I knew what her newest discovery was and that she would end up going to the police with her knowledge."

Madame Dubois made no attempt at hiding her contempt as she thought back to the confrontation with Megan and stated, "Finding the monkeys was one thing; I could have easily explained them to the authorities by saying that my next window scene would involve monkeys. But she made the correct connection regarding the current display, and that was evidence I could not get rid of in a hurry. I knew that she needed to be silenced. I made a threatening remark, hoping that she would do nothing for a day or two."

Huber interrupted, "What was the remark?"

"Oh, something to the effect that she'd better keep her mouth shut or her days would be numbered."

"I see."

Madame Dubois continued, "I was pretty sure that she would wait until after the premiere to go to the police, because she was preoccupied with her performance coming up the next night. I also knew that on that same Friday evening she would be kept busy with a dress rehearsal. So I didn't have much time to form a plan, but time enough."

She paused and took a sip from her coffee. At that exact moment Andi leaned forward and with a quick jerky movement managed to bump the other's arm, making her spill most of the beverage.

Andi cried out, "So clumsy of me; I'm terribly sorry, ma'am!" She jumped out of her seat. "Let me help you clean up."

Madame Dubois was already on her feet and ordered, "Sit down, I'll take care of it," and left the showroom area. Seconds later she came back with a rag and wiped her chair and the floor dry.

Andi seemed full of remorse and said again, "I'm so sorry." And eyeing Madame Dubois's nearly empty cup, she offered her own, saying, "Here, take mine please; I haven't touched it yet."

"Thanks, but no. I'll just get myself another," and she was gone down the hallway again.

Huber quickly got to her feet, grabbed Andi's cup and her own and tiptoed over to a Philodendron plant that sat on a corner shelf. She promptly poured a generous amount of their coffees into the pot. When the owner of *Le Monde Fashion* came back with her own new brew, she found the two investigators relaxed in their seats, pretending to sip theirs.

Chapter 48

Madame Dubois asked, "Where was I?"

Huber replied, "You were saying that you felt pressed for time to form a plan."

"Right. So I got busy. Chad had been working on making a bomb that was easily set off by remote control from a cell phone. In fact, he was fanatical about it to the point that I had started to worry about him. He even went out to the desert with his creation and did a dry run. More than once, he begged our leader to find a use for it on one of the burglar jobs, but his wish was not taken seriously. So I clued Chad in on our problem with Megan and explained that I'd found a use for his bomb after all.

"Then I figured out all the details and bought the orchid. All he had to do was install the bomb into the flower pot and program it to his cell phone. Don't ask me how that is done; I don't understand the technical part of it. I made up a bogus flower shop and had him bring the thing to the back entrance of the Cubbyhole, pretending he was making a delivery from the florist. I asked Chad if there was a relatively long stretch of time when Megan was on stage and he was not, and sure enough, the last scene was perfect for our purpose. I won't bore you ladies with the exact details, but my game plan worked with precision, just like your Swiss watch, Madame Huber!"

Andi put in, "Mrs. Huber already figured out a scenario of how it could've been done on the day we interviewed the actors. I reckon your boyfriend followed your brainchild in a similar way."

Madame Dubois pointed out, "Yes, it was my brainchild, but don't forget, Chad did the actual killing with his bomb!"

Huber took a mock-sip of coffee and then remarked, "Hiding the stolen gems in plain view in your window displays took real genius to carry out."

"Yes, I'm proud of that."

"You changed your displays often. What happened to the jewels once they left your window?"

"I only kept them while they were hot; eventually they went to a dealer."

Huber had yawned a couple of times already and now Andi did likewise and asked, "Is it gettin' hot in here?"

Madame Dubois replied, "Not really, I have the thermostat set at 70 degrees."

Then Huber asked, "Another thing I've been wondering about, how many people are in your group of thieves - - assuming that there is a group?"

"We have seven members."

"And each has a different function within the gang?"

"You could say that. Each member has his or her own expertise. Except for Chad, I don't know anybody of the team personally. We are nameless within the group and are referred to by numbers only."

"You mentioned a leader. Does he mastermind the burglaries and give the orders?"

"Yes he does."

Huber purposely slowed her speech pretending to get drowsy and said, "Did he instruct you to get rid of Megan?"

"No, he didn't know about it until after the fact. He was actually angry at Chad and me for taking care of her, since he doesn't approve of violence." She shrugged, "The imbecile didn't seem to realize that it was necessary, and that we did the entire group a favor. Imagine that!"

Huber's eyelids flickered - - then slowly closed as she leaned back in her chair - - and with a final little sigh her entire body relaxed into a reclining position.

Andi inquired, "Boss, are you all right?"

Madame Dubois said, "Do you suppose she has taken ill?"

"Could be. I'm feelin' mighty strange myself. Ya didn't slip us a Mickey, now did ya? That coffee tasted - -"

Andi did not finish her sentence and slumped forward, seemingly oblivious to the world.

Chapter 49

Finally! Madame Dubois thought. It took forever for those sleeping pills to kick in. Now at long last the two women were in a sound slumber and she had plenty of time to prepare for what needed to be done. She would not enjoy what came next, but the investigators had left her no other choice. She hoped that they would not feel a thing, but should they become semi-conscious and fight her, at least it would be over quickly. Before she went to her workshop to make sure that all was handy, she glanced at the pair. Andi was still slumped over and R. A. Huber had her head tilted back and rested one hand against the armrest of the chair, the other behind her back. The purse sat at her feet.

In her workshop, the industrial size dolly for transporting props and mannequins stood ready in the far corner of the room. She eyed it speculatively and thought; it will serve the purpose. That the detective showed up was no surprise, however, she had not anticipated having to deal with the young assistant. This meant double the work but she could handle it. She would have to wait a few hours before she dared make the transportation. The wait with two corpses in her boutique would be nerve wracking, but she did not want to dwell on that right now.

She smiled to herself as she pictured the bodies being found at the Cubbyhole - - Chad's territory, not hers. That should keep the police on *his* back. As for me, I'll deny everything; my word against his. After tonight, there will be no evidence to tie me to Megan's murder. I'll have plenty of time to rearrange my window display while I wait until after midnight to dispose of the two women.

It was time to get organized, she decided. First she grabbed two surgical gloves from a box on the lower shelf and eased her hands into them. Next she went over to the cupboard and took out four industrial garbage bags and placed them on the dolly. Then she pulled two smaller plastic bags and two strings, already cut to size, out of a drawer and was prepared to go back to her charges.

Madame Dubois pushed the dolly along the hallway to the showroom area where she found the two women exactly the way she had left them. Andi was slumped over and Huber's position had not changed. One of Huber's hands was in plain view, the other behind her back. The purse at her feet looked somewhat different. She told herself, you're imagining things, Annette!

She resolved to take care of Andi first and walked over to the redhead's chair. She pushed her head into an upright position and sat her body straight until it leaned against the backrest. Andi had her eyes closed and did not move a muscle. Then Madame Dubois pulled the plastic bag over her head and placed the string around the neck.

She was in the process of pulling the string tight when the command came, "Hold it right there!"

She shrieked and let go of the string, staring at a cocked .25 pistol which Huber aimed at the exact center of her forehead.

Without taking her eyes off the antagonist Huber asked, "Andi, are you all right?"

"Sure thing, boss," she replied, yanking the bag off her head and rubbing her neck.

Recovering from the initial shock Madame Dubois questioned, "That thing is loaded, yes?"

"You bet it is, and I mean business!"

Keeping her eyes on Madame Dubois and never relaxing her aim she said, "Andi, call the police, please."

"Yes ma'am. 911?"

"No, get in touch with the homicide detective handling Megan's murder case. His name is Lieutenant Olson. Sergeant Wolf gave us his number."

"Gotcha. I have it in memory mode," and she made the call.

Huber ordered, "Take your seat, Madame Dubois. While we wait for the officers to arrive, I'll make sure that you behave. Don't think for a moment that I'm giving you a chance to get rid of the evidence in our coffee cups, nor the incriminating gems in your display window."

After Madame Dubois was taken away in handcuffs, Lieutenant Olson and one of his minions stayed behind, addressing Huber and Andi.

He said, "It's getting late; we can take down your formal statements now, or you can come over to the station tomorrow."

Huber stated, "I would like to give you a full account now as there are more people involved." And she informed him of Chad Lindhurst's role in the murder, as well as the two culprits' connection to the monkey tail burglars.

Chad was arrested on the same night.

Chapter 50

The grilling of Madame Dubois and Chad Lindhurst was in full swing. The two were held in separate interrogation rooms, and Lieutenant Olson had made it clear that a lesser sentence could be negotiated if they cooperated. The questioning of Chad proved fruitless; he kept quiet, did not admit to anything, and asked to have an attorney present. Madame Dubois, on the other hand, spilled the beans. She squealed on Chad, accusing him of Megan's murder while playing down her own part of instigating and plotting it.

Having gone over the specifics of the murder, the lieutenant stated, "Now let's talk about the other matter. We know all about your involvement with the monkey tail burglar gang. Who are the other members of the group besides you and Mr. Lindhurst?"

"I don't know them," Madame Dubois replied.

"Don't play dumb. Give us their names. Remember what I told you about a lesser sentence if you cooperate."

"I honestly don't know their names," and she explained how the members' identities had been kept secret and that they only referred to one another by numbers during their meetings.

Lieutenant Olson ordered, "Tell me about the meetings."

She was eager to comply and divulged the monkey tail burglars' meeting place, as well as the purpose and procedure of the meetings in detail.

He paid keen attention and then asked, "When is your next meeting scheduled?"

"In about two months; I don't know the exact date. Member One will contact us via the Yahoo group."

There was a long silence while he mulled over her information. Madame Dubois nervously tapped her foot against the leg of the table, waiting.

Seated across from her, Lieutenant Olson leaned back in his chair and closed his eyes, forming a plan of action. He finally thought, Yes, it may work. I'll have to clear it with my superiors, which should be no problem if I handle them right.

After what seemed an eternity to Madame Dubois, he said, "We'll keep your and Mr. Lindhurst's arrest under wraps for the time being. I'll make sure that there is no leak of it to the press, TV stations, or anyone else."

He eyed her keenly and said, "I need your full cooperation in order for my strategy to work."

"You have it," she assured him.

"I'm not worried about keeping Mr. Lindhurst's confinement a secret; except for his acting buddies, I doubt that many people will miss seeing him. It won't be hard to come up with a plausible excuse for his absence at work and the theater group. In your case it might be trickier. How are we going to explain the closing of your store to your employees and clientele?"

Motivated to showing her cooperation she burst out, "Leave it to me. I'll think of something."

Lieutenant Olson studied her for some time. He finally said, "Okay, here is what I want you to do," and he told her the part of the game plan that involved her participation.

Chapter 51

At the end of June, Member One called his last meeting to order.

He said, "I see Member Six is not present. We'll proceed without him then. Let's hear your reports. You first, Member Seven."

The latter stated, "It took some cunning negotiation, but I was able to cut us some great deals. I initially- -"

Member One cut him short and ordered, "Stop the self-promotion and give us the figures."

"As you wish." Member Seven opened his folder and read from his notes, "The Woodward watercolor cleared $56,000.00, the Lladro figurines $8,000.00, and I was able to get an excellent price of $6,500.00 for the Tiffany Favrile vase. That comes to a total of $70,500.00."

"Thank you."

He turned to Member Five and said, "Now give us your account of the gem sale. In my estimation the total should amount to at least $130,000.00."

Madame Dubois stammered, "Sorry, but I was not able to complete the transaction."

Annoyed, Member One shot back, "Then give us what deals you've made so far."

She bit her lip and murmured, "The jewels have not been put in circulation yet."

"What! Didn't you get the green light command to go ahead? Speak up woman; what prompted you to hold back?"

Madame Dubois turned bright red and was spared an answer as the door flew open and Lieutenant Olson and his men burst in, their guns at the ready, shouting, "Police! Everyone stay in your seats and remove your masks!"

EPILOGUE

One day at the beginning of November, Sergeant John Wolf stopped by R. A. Huber's office for a visit.

She looked up from her computer, took off her glasses, and got to her feet, exclaiming, "Sergeant Wolf, what a pleasant surprise!"

He took her extended hand firmly into his and said, "I hope you're not too busy to talk to an old friend."

"I can always make time for you, Sergeant," she said, and motioned him into the client chair while settling back into hers. "How was your Rhine river cruise?"

"We had a great time and were extremely lucky with the weather; not a rainy day! My wife talked me into another trip later and that's why I missed the Dubois/Lindhurst murder trial."

"I'm glad you're enjoying your retirement."

"That's a fact. I keep far away from crime these days," he remarked with a chuckle. Then he cleared his throat and the dark eyes beneath his bushy brows regarded her in earnest as he said, "I talked with Owen and Eileen the other day. They are grateful for what you did for them and asked me to thank you."

"Andi and I just did our job. Besides; the Maguires already sent me a touching thank you note when they paid the bill."

"That's right, you have an assistant now. How is she working out?"

"Andi is a breath of fresh air! You'd get a kick out of her, I'm sure. And what's more, she is a good investigator. I've come to rely on her in the last three years."

He got back to his subject and said, "Owen and Eileen came down for the trial and heard your testimony. According to them, your statements on the witness stand are what nailed the case for the jury. If it hadn't been for you, Megan's murder might have never been solved."

"I think the credit goes to Megan herself. She clearly pointed the killer out with her last line."

"Nobody seemed to have noticed the significance of that line at the time."

"I'm sure Madame Dubois understood! Most likely, she was on needles for a couple of days, but when no one made the connection, she assumed that she was home free and relaxed."

"Owen related the trial to me and what came to light during the court procedures. I never met the woman, but that Madame Dubois sounds like a cold-blooded customer."

"She sure is," Huber replied, "while full of charm and charisma on the surface."

He remarked, "The woman took a big risk with displaying the stolen jewels in her window."

"Not really. The gems were disguised in many ways." And she explained, "At the holiday scene, for example, the diamonds on the brilliant star were mounted between glass pebbles, and the gems in the pirate display were scattered among fake jewelry in the treasure chest. She cleverly placed the real stones amid the imitations. Also, Madame Dubois was always behind with her window scenes. In other words, the latest booty was not showcased in the store window until a month later."

The sergeant remarked, "A clever woman; too bad she used her talents for crime." Then he asked, "What was she planning to do with you and Andi? Owen wasn't clear on that."

"She laced our coffees with enough sleeping pills to make a 200 pound person snore, and after we'd have been out cold, her plan was to suffocate us by pulling plastic bags over our heads."

"I know that part, but what was she going to do with your bodies?"

"Her idea was to plant us at the Cubbyhole Theater's doorstep, trying to incriminate either Chad Lindhurst or Adriana Rippling, or both. We managed to get her all worked up over some alleged infidelities of her boyfriend, which helped to make her unscrupulous where he was concerned. She had heavy-duty plastic bags and an industrial size dolly ready for our transportation. I think that she was prepared for me to show up at her store with accusations, but seeing Andi at my side must have been a shock. So having to dispose of two corpses would have been an additional burden to her, but she is spry and strong for her petite size."

He commented, "The woman would have taken an enormous risk by transporting your bodies in that fashion. How could she be sure that there wouldn't be any witnesses?"

"Actually, pulling the dolly from her store to her truck and loading the heavy plastic sacks into the vehicle would have caused no suspicion. Neighbors were used to seeing her with a dolly pulling props and scenery items for her window displays at all hours of the night. Granted, at the Cubbyhole end it would have been trickier, but I presume that she'd have waited until one or two in the morning, when traffic was at its lightest, before attempting her maneuver. And in my opinion, Madame Dubois enjoyed the thrill of taking risks."

He reflected a moment on what he had learned and then inquired, "What do you suppose would have happened if you and your assistant declined to drink the coffee?"

"That occurred to me too and I think she would have refused to say another word and shown us the door. She might have had a vague plan B on how to silence us in that event. The woman was good at making last-minute schemes to save her skin when unexpected problems popped up."

Sergeant Wolf asked, "What about the gang of thieves? How did their justice pan out?"

With a smirk Huber replied, "You must have been out of town again recently when they held the separate trial of the monkey tail burglars."

"Believe it or not, I was home sick with the stomach flu and missed it. I read about the trial later, but the article in the paper lacked many details. Did you sit through it?"

"Not the entire trial, but I witnessed part of it. The monkey tail burglars are a fascinating group of people."

"Don't keep me in suspense!"

"Okay, I'll tell you all I know about them. First off, only Madame Dubois and Chad Lindhurst were responsible for Megan's murder; the rest had nothing to do with it. Except for those two, people within the gang did not know one another by name but were simply referred to as Member One, Two, Three, and so forth. There were seven of them and Member One was their mastermind and leader. I should also mention that aside from Chad, none of the actors or anyone else associated with the amateur theater group was a member of the monkey tail burglars."

The Sergeant remarked, "That was one of the things left unclear in the paper."

She continued, "Member One originally handpicked his team and did extended background research on all before asking them to join. He scrutinized many applicants until he ended up with what he considered a perfect crew.

It was all done online, and even though he knew their names and positions, they did not know who he was nor did they know one another. In my opinion, keeping his subordinates nameless and without contact among each other outside the burglar jobs was essential to his success.

"The only exception to that rule was our two murderers. When Member One asked Madame Dubois on board, she suggested he also make Chad Lindhurst a member, since he would come in handy as a safecracker. Against Member One's better judgment he agreed, as he certainly had a use for Chad's expertise. It took him a long time to get his group together, making sure they were top-drawer in their respective fields. One of his criteria was that they had a solid and above-board day job; another, that they could follow orders and be trusted; and most importantly, that none had a criminal record."

"What was his hook to get them to join?"

"He promised thrilling adventures with some profit as a bonus."

"One can look at it in that way, I suppose."

"As I said, it took him months to form his team; he rejected a slew of people before he finally chose his six experts. They held secret meetings in a hotel conference room which Member One rented on a monthly basis where he informed them of their next heist and discussed the details. If he needed to get in touch with them between meetings, it was done via a Yahoo group, so all could stay anonymous."

"Do you know what each member's profession was and consequently their specific abilities?"

Huber met his brown steady eyes with amusement and answered, "I was just getting to that! I might not have them in the correct order, but here goes: Member One is Vice President of a major bank. He was the band of thieves' brain and ruler, giving all the orders. He had a knack for plotting each heist to perfection. As a banker, he easily obtained the approximate worth of a potential victim. His excellent organizing skills, as well as the ability to manage people, served him well for his purpose. Member Two, a woman, is a gem expert and her daytime job was with a prominent dealer of precious stones and metals. She determined the approximate value of each piece of jewelry on the spot.

"Member Three was their art expert. He was able to distinguish the authentic works of any particular artist from the fakes. I can't remember what his profession is, but he comes from old-money and is an aristocrat who mingled with the rich and famous, ferreting out their habits and tastes in works of art. He is originally from England and never wavered from his high-brow demeanor while giving testimony. Member Four's occupation escapes me at the moment too. He was a former gymnast and a wizard with ropes and climbed trees like a monkey, hence the group's symbolism with monkeys.

"Member Five is none other than *Le Monde Fashion's* Madame Dubois. As we know, she displayed the stolen gems in her window while they were hot. She also got tips from her clientele as far as ownership of certain pieces of jewelry and works of art. And Member Six was our notorious Chad Lindhurst. He worked as an electronics technician with a local firm and was the team's safe cracker and explosives expert."

Huber beamed when she added, "His background was no news to me when mentioned in the trial. I had checked it out months before for myself. He had trained as an explosives expert in Operation Desert Storm. And last, we have Member Seven, owner of an import/export business who often shipped merchandise out of the country. He was a frequent flyer abroad himself. You can easily guess who was in charge of dispensing the loot."

"What an operation! And this went on over a year on a monthly basis?"

"More or less. Madame Dubois and Member Three provided easy access to information about the daily habits of the targeted rich and famous. I think the reason Member One's scheme worked so well was that the members had no connection to one another in their every day lives. The exception was Madame Dubois and Chad, who in the end let him down. He mentioned in the trial that when adding them to his team, he had ordered the two never to get in touch with each other outside their monthly meetings. I have the feeling he had no idea they were lovers. Member One also testified that he had held everyone on his team to a non-violence code. He felt that the two had sold him out by killing Megan."

Sergeant Wolf said, "None of these people seemed to be in dire straights for money, so they did these robberies just for fun?"

Huber nodded. "I believe it became an addiction. Some folks jump from one extreme sport to another to get their thrills, and the monkey tail burglars craved the risk, excitement, and danger of these night jobs. I think that they regarded the profit from their ill-gotten gains as dessert."

"Do they have spouses and families?"

"Some do, and others are single. Member One, the banker, has a wife and three teenage kids."

"How was Lieutenant Olson able to catch all the members since their names were unknown?"

"You do know about the raid, right?"

"What raid?"

So Huber told all about how Madame Dubois, who was out on bail at the time, led the police to the gang's meeting place at the hotel in Pasadena in the hope of a lesser sentence. She disclosed that Lieutenant Olson and his subordinates raided the place, arresting every member of the gang. She also explained that Chad Lindhurst never admitted to his crime and claimed to know nothing about any monkey tail burglars.

After a pause the Sergeant said, "So what was their verdict?"

"They all pleaded guilty, throwing themselves at the mercy of the court. I can't recall how many years of prison they were charged with; it varied with each member. The banker is serving the most time, no question about that." And Huber added, "When the judge asked him what his reason was for masterminding the robberies, he answered, 'When dealing with a midlife crisis, some people take up car racing, get into extreme sports, or have an affair. I chose plotting burglaries.'"

"What about the stolen goods?"

"Some were recovered, like the jewels still in Madame Dubois's possession. However, a substantial portion of the booty has not come to light, and I suspect that it never will. The stolen items have been dispersed underground, either here or abroad."

"So a guilty verdict was not much compensation for the burglary victims."

"Oh, there are civil lawsuits pending, and the thieves will have to reach deep into their wallets before all is set and done."

Then Sergeant Wolf said, "As for our main two jailbirds, I may not have been present at their trial, but the result was all over the news. Chad Lindhurst is locked up for life without parole. Madame Dubois got 30 years, with a possibility of parole after 15 years. I think that both deserved a life sentence. In addition to the burglaries, they are responsible for the ruthless killing of Megan and, in Madame's case, the attempted murder of you and Andi. But sometimes good police work calls for compromise. Also, by the time Dubois steps out of prison she'll be an old lady. I'd say she got her due."

Huber suddenly had a faraway look in her eyes and then shared, "I have an inkling that Megan would proclaim: *'Justice is ultimately served!'*"

R. A. Huber Mysteries by Alice Zogg

Murder at the Cubbyhole
Revamp Camp
Final Stop Albuquerque
The Fall of Optimum House
The Lonesome Autocrat
Tracking Backward
Turn the Joker Around
Reaching Checkmate

Available at www.amazon.com,
www.barnesandnoble.com
and other vendors.